# THE SMASHED MAN OF DREAD END

# THE SMASHED MAN OF DREAD END

## J.W. OCKER

**HARPER**

*An Imprint of HarperCollinsPublishers*

*To Esme and Hazel, the real Noe and Len.*
*And to Olive. I'll have to find another monster for you to fight.*

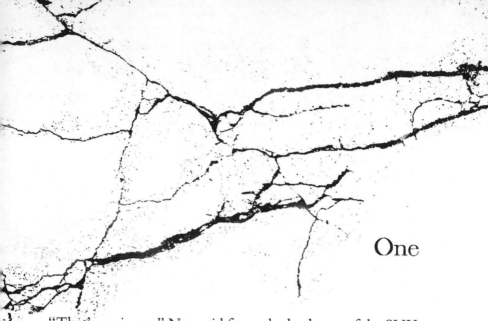

# One

"That's ominous," Noe said from the back seat of the SUV.

"Om-eee-nus," repeated Len.

Noelle Wiley glanced at her three-year-old sister. Lenore was squeezing a stuffed anteater to her chest and straining against the straps of a car seat covered in dried yogurt glops and apple juice stains. Noe wrinkled her nose and scrunched closer to the SUV door. "Quiet, Len," she said.

"Don't talk to your sister like that," said Mom from the driver's seat.

"And don't freak out. It's not ominous. That's just another name for a cul-de-sac." Dad was in the front passenger seat, poking at his phone like he was trying to get it to pay attention to him.

The topic of conversation was a diamond-shaped

yellow sign on the side of the road. On it, in blocky black letters, were two words: DEAD END.

But Noe wasn't talking about the sign. She was talking about what was spray-painted on the sign. Squeezed between the first two letters of "DEAD" was an R in sparkly black paint, turning the phrase into DREAD END. The R was deformed, with the hump at the top longer and thinner than it should have been.

As the SUV slowly passed the sign and turned the corner, Dad continued. "You're going to love living at the end of a cul-de-sac, Noe. The street is your own private blacktop. You can bike on it or play basketball on it or cover it in chalk drawings or lie in the middle of it without worrying that cars are going to run you over."

"She can't lie in the middle of it," said Mom.

"She can if we put out one of those signs that say Slow Children. Our children are pretty slow." Noe's phone vibrated in her pocket, and she fished it out to see that Dad had sent her a wink emoji.

Her parents had been handling her like an egg carton full of tiny time bombs since they had told her they were moving. They had lived in the old house for all of Noe's life. And now, at thirteen, she would be facing the terrors of a new place.

What her parents didn't know was that she didn't care

that they were moving. It wasn't like they were moving to another state. Or even to another town. They were staying in Osshua, just moving to the north end of it. That meant a new house and a new school district, but that was fine. Noe was done with her old school, anyway. The jerk-to-friend ratio there was pretty high, and her best friend had stopped being one.

Len, sensing that her sister's thoughts had gone to unpleasant places, shifted the anteater and peeled a mummified french fry off the lining of her car seat. She offered it to her sister. Noe scrunched tighter against the door, pressing her cheek against the window, which was cool despite the summer outside. Len gave up and pretended to feed the fry to her anteater.

As the car rounded the curve, passing a less ominous green sign labeled TOTTER COURT, the entire dead end—Noe hated the phrase "cul-de-sac," it sounded like a bad word—appeared through the front window of the SUV.

The neighborhood sat at the bottom of a ravine like it was pressed into the ground by a giant thumb. The ravine wall rose about thirty feet behind the houses on one side of the block, but then gradually lowered around the curve of the dead end until the wall disappeared behind the houses on the other side of the road. Between the backyards of the neighborhood and the base of the ravine grew a thin forest of trees.

Their new house was near the dead end of the dead end street, on the side of the road where the ravine was tallest. The house was a red saltbox with black shutters and a black door. On top of the roof was a metal weather vane, shaped like a walking Pilgrim, that had aged into a pale green. The house looked like it dated to colonial times, but it had been built only a few decades ago. Most of the houses in the neighborhood were like that, built to reflect an older New England. On one side of their new house was a gray house similar to their own, and on the other side was a forested lot that had never been cleared. The closest house on that side was a white one at the very tip of the dead end. It was set halfway up the ravine, which was a gentle slope at that point.

Noe's new school was somewhere behind that white house, on the other side of the forested slope. She could walk there in minutes. That meant no bus, no parents dropping her off—and sleeping in until the last possible moment. Another reason to be happy with this move. But summer was no time for school thoughts.

What Noe wasn't happy with was helping Dad carry in all the moving boxes from the rental truck that was parked in their driveway. The furniture had been carried into the house yesterday by the movers Dad had hired, but he wanted to save money on the boxes and smaller items. Len was too young to help, so that left her and Mom and Dad to lug boxes. Which they started doing immediately after they arrived.

The house was larger than their old house. Two floors and a basement, four bedrooms, two bathrooms. The first floor was laid out in a circle, so you could run around forever without hitting a wall. The bedrooms were all on the second floor.

Noe dropped a box full of clothes onto the wide pine planks of her bedroom floor, wiped her forehead, and looked around. Blank walls and a bare floor and two windows. Soon her dog posters would cover the walls and her furniture would cover the floor. She stared out one of the windows. A large backyard— perfect for a dog— stretched flat and green and almost featureless except for a large stone-ringed firepit to one side. The yard ended at that thin strip of forest at the base of the ravine. Behind their house, the forest thickened and continued through a gap in the ravine wall and into a large forest preserve. Even though they were still in town, only a mile from the nearest grocery store, in fact, it felt like they were in the middle of nowhere. When Noe looked out the windows in the back of the house, it looked like they lived in a forest. When she looked out the windows at the front of the house, it looked like they lived in a neighborhood. It had to be the strangest street in town.

Noe could barely make out the face of the ravine through all the foliage and couldn't at all make out the houses perched atop the ravine, which faced the opposite direction. Dad said that during winter, when the trees were bare, they'd have a clear view of the backs of those houses. And that hopefully everybody up there used curtains. Noe herself couldn't wait for fall, when the maple and oak and birch trees would burn into bright reds and oranges and yellows around them. At the old house, they'd only had a few scraggly bushes and an ugly telephone pole in their yard.

As she walked back downstairs and into the living room, she passed Mom, who was pushing a hand truck stacked with three boxes, each labeled DINING ROOM. "Looks like you have a welcoming committee outside," said Mom, stopping in front of Noe.

"What?"

"There are kids out there. Looks like they're waiting to meet you. Go be neighborly." She angled the handcart to let Noe pass. "Don't worry. I'll save you some boxes to carry."

Noe walked over to one of the windows that

overlooked the front lawn. The house was set far enough back from the street that it felt separated from the rest of the neighborhood.

At the edge of the lawn, like they were afraid of trampling the grass, stood three girls. They weren't moving or talking or looking around. They just stared at the house. "Creepy," Noe said to herself.

"I bet their eyeballs are completely black," said Dad, making Noe jump. He laughed. "Go say hi. Find out if any of their parents are accountants. I need one who'll give me a good neighbor discount."

Noe did go outside, but not to meet the girls. They seemed too strange to her. Instead, she grabbed another box off the moving truck. As she turned to walk inside, she saw movement in the group. One of the girls broke away and started walking up the driveway to her. Noe held the box like a shield in front of her. It said BATHROOM on it.

The girl's dark hair was woven into tight braids tipped with red and white plastic beads and then gathered into a loose ponytail. Around her neck was a piece of twine holding a smooth stone with a hole in it. She stood there and didn't say anything, acting like Noe had walked up to her.

"Hi," Noe finally said. "I'm Noelle."

The girl stared at the dark asphalt under her feet. "Don't go in the basement of your house at night." She said it really fast, as if she had been holding it in for hours. "Your little sister either." The girl nodded at Len, who had followed Noe outside and was peeking shyly around Noe's leg at the new girl like she'd fallen in love with her.

"What?" asked Noe.

"Don't go in the basement at night." The girl turned around and ran back to the group, who immediately dispersed in different directions like they were a rack of pool balls.

"That's ominous," said Noe.

"Om-eee-nus," repeated Len.

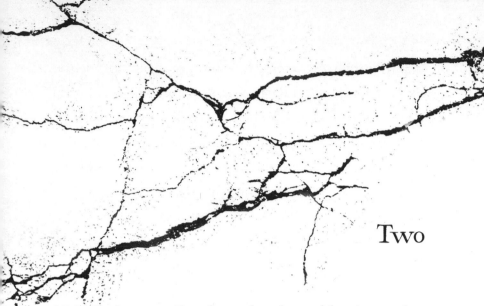

# Two

Noe's bed was a pile of wood and metal leaning against the far wall of her new room. She lay on a mattress on the floor. Dad hadn't put the beds together yet, so the whole family was roughing it. The air seemed dusty close to the floor, and she felt as if somebody was about to step on her at any moment.

The quiet in the house was more bothersome than sleeping on the floor. The road in front of her old house had been busy. There were always cars driving by and people outside talking. But at this house, nothing. Between the lack of sound and the heat, it was suffocating. She got up and cracked a window. More than a stray breeze, she needed something to break the bubble of silence that was pushing at her ears. But out there, it was still and quiet. Wait. Not quiet. It took her a few moments of concentration, but she finally heard bugs chirping in a strange, unending cadence, like the forest was full of static. But that was hardly real noise. Car engines and ambulance sirens were real noise.

Noe wasn't trying to fall asleep, though. She looked at her phone. It sat angled in its charging stand, beaming the time at her in glowing white characters: 11:15 p.m. Her parents were more than likely deep asleep after the manual labor of moving boxes all day. People with desk jobs shouldn't try to move an entire house by themselves.

Noe got up and stuck her feet into fuzzy green slippers, threw on a purple robe, and tiptoed down the hallway. She peeked into Len's room. A decapitated unicorn nightlight showed Len asleep, her arms wrapped around a stuffed lemur. On the other end of the hallway, her parents' door was open, but the room was completely dark inside. She could hear Dad snoring loudly and wondered how Mom slept next to him.

She felt her way down the stairs to the first floor. It was difficult going. The unfamiliar space was filled with boxes, and she had no clue where all the light switches were. She walked around the rooms, banging her shins a few times, and then finally heard the slap of vinyl against her slippers that told her she was in the kitchen. She found a switch near the sink and flipped it.

A loud metal roar made Noe's insides go cold in terror.

Then she realized that she had hit the garbage disposal switch. She hit the switch again and waited a few seconds in the darkness to see if the noise had woken anybody up. Apparently Dad's snores beat the noise of the garbage disposal, because she didn't hear any movement upstairs. She flipped a second switch beside the sink, and the kitchen appeared.

So did the basement door.

The portal to the place she wasn't supposed to go into after dark.

The door to the basement looked . . . absolutely ordinary. Well, not absolutely. It was black with a black doorknob and an old-fashioned keyhole, so by itself maybe a little eerie, but all the doors in the house were black, just like the shutters on the outside of the house. But it was still just a door. A slab of black-painted wood beside the pantry.

Noe looked behind her out the large kitchen window above the sink. During the day, its view was of the forest at the bottom of the ravine. Now, at night, the window was a black square set above the kitchen sink, a dark mirror that she saw herself reflected in. Herself and the door.

The house had darkened inside long before the sun set. Dad said it was because the ravine and all the trees blocked the light when the sun was low. Whatever the reason, the house felt like it was in permanent dusk most of the day.

Like they were in a cabin in the woods. Mom was already planning on buying about twenty lamps for the house. She had the spots for each one marked on the floor with masking-tape X's even before the movers had carried in the furniture.

Noe looked at herself one more time in the black mirror of the window and then turned the knob on the basement door, which felt colder than it should have in the summer heat. The latch clicked, and she swung open the door. It didn't even creak.

She could see the first few rough wooden steps, and then the rest of the stairway was swallowed by void. This would be her first time in the basement. She hadn't had time to check it out all day, and she had only been in the house one other time, during the house inspection. She had spent almost the entire time running around the yard making sure it was a dog yard. Dad had promised to get them a dog once they lived in a house with a big enough yard, and she was going to hold him to that. Besides, when Dad had gone downstairs with the inspector, he had returned with stories about furnaces and laundry machines. Boring stuff.

She turned on the light and slowly descended the stairs, knowing she was giving whatever was supposed to be hiding down there the advantage of getting ready for her. She wasn't scared. Well, she was scared, but there were different types of scared. Noe knew a lot of the types. The type she was feeling right now was something like uncertainty and anticipation. It was an adventurous scared. She needed to show those girls who were trying to prank her that she wasn't an easy target. No random girl with a rock around her neck was going to tell Noe what she couldn't do in her own house.

As soon as she hit the floor of the basement, the temperature seemed to drop twenty degrees. Being underground and insulated by thick walls meant it was always cool down there. Stranger than the temperature, though, was that there wasn't any basement floor.

Her fuzzy green slippers were standing on dirt.

It wasn't like outside dirt. Nothing grew in it. Not a single dandelion or blade of grass. It hadn't seen rain or sunshine since the house had been built atop it. And it was packed hard. Like concrete. She could probably bounce a Super Ball on it easily. Noe doubted that she could even dig up the dirt with her fingernails. She cringed at the thought of the dirt bending back her nails. She wondered what was in the dirt under the house. Worms? Groundhogs? An old cemetery?

The basement was a single large room that ran the entire footprint of the house. It had four windows, but they were mere slivers of glass stuck against the ceiling of the basement. They were shiny black rectangles right now, and during the day probably weren't much better. Since they were at ground level outside, they must always be blocked by grass. It was probably worse in the winter, when they would be whited out by snow. All the light in the room came from the three bare bulbs screwed into the wooden rafters that were low enough that her father probably had to duck under them. But the light bulbs did little to dispel the murkiness.

Looking around, she didn't see any movement. Not a mouse. Not a bug. In a corner of the basement, in a small alcove below the steps, were the washer and dryer, set atop a concrete slab. Against the wall to her right were stacks of boxes, each one marked with sloppily written words in black marker. Her name appeared on a couple of them. Probably stuff from when she was a kid that had been stored in the basement at the old house. The only other things in the basement were the boxy furnace and the tall water heater, which stood in the middle of the floor on their own concrete slab. The metal cylinder of the water heater tank was about five feet tall and surrounded by piping and valves and meters the purposes of which were a mystery to her, a mystery she didn't ever care to solve. As long as she was able to have a hot shower every day.

But it was the walls of the basement that really creeped her out.

They were built of giant rough slabs of rock, each one almost as big as Len. It reminded her of Egyptian pyramid stones, except gray, with rough contours that looked like they'd been shaped with ancient tools. A thin line of cement kept them all together, although alarming cracks wended their way through the rocks and mortar like rivers on a map.

The place looked like a castle dungeon. It only needed iron manacles dangling from the rocks, and maybe a skeleton in the corner.

She circled the water heater to see what was on the other side. Nothing but more packed dirt. More slabs of rocks. More cracks in the wall, including a vicious-looking one that started at the top, near the rafters, and then zigzagged all the way to the bottom. It looked like earthquake damage, but this area didn't have earthquakes. Not that she knew of.

The basement was empty and musty, without a single hiding place for anything. But it did feel different down here. Like the molecules in the air were thickly packed. The atmosphere of the basement pressed the sides of her head like headphones that were too tight.

She didn't like it down here.

But not enough to warn somebody not to come down here. Had those kids been in this basement? Had they known the people who lived here before? Her parents had bought this place because it was a bigger house than what they had and very affordable. They weren't even looking for a new house. It had come onto the market suddenly. Noe had been the one to find it. Not that she was into real estate. She was just trying to figure out how big a yard you would need for an average-sized dog. She had come across it online and liked the red color and the flat metal man on the roof and the old look of the whole thing. Dad was standing nearby, so she showed it to him. When he saw it, his face almost dropped off his skull. She'd never seen him so surprised. Apparently it was a really good deal.

A little more than a month later, they were living in it. It was a sudden and strange move. But the house was definitely worth sudden and strange. Even if it did have a creepy basement and creepy neighbors.

She looked up at the night-colored rectangles at the top of the walls. Her imagination painted in a pair of shoes in one of the windows, like a stranger was standing beside the house in the dark. Between that image and the image of the buried dead beneath her, she realized it was time to leave the basement. Her imagination was lashing out at her for not going to sleep.

Noe walked back to the stairs and looked up into the bright rectangle that was the kitchen . . . and almost jumped out of her fuzzy green slippers.

A small form was silhouetted in the door.

"Werewolves," the small shape said softly.

"You jerk, Len. You scared me to death. What are you doing up?" Noe squinted at her sister. Len was wearing a bright green onesie, her bottom swollen by a diaper and her arms strangling her lemur.

"Werewolves down there," Len mumbled.

"You think there are werewolves everywhere," said Noe. Len was afraid of the dark. She made Noe turn on the overhead light in the SUV when they were driving at night, and she wouldn't even step outside onto a porch if it was dusk. They'd had to cut trick-or-treating short last year because Len couldn't handle it. Not even a plastic pumpkin full of candy could tempt her to stay out. She said it was because there were werewolves in the dark. That was Noe's fault. She had let Len watch a werewolf movie with her one night. It was an old one, all black-and-white with fake fog and even faker trees. And now werewolves were Len's bogeymen.

Len muttered something else that wasn't "werewolves," but that Noe didn't understand. And that was when she realized that her little sister wasn't really talking to her. Wasn't really looking at her. That she was wobbling a little.

Len was sleepwalking.

Noe's heart dropped as she imagined her sister falling down the stairs. She dashed up them two at a time and grabbed Len in her arms before her sister tumbled down those hard steps to that hard dirt floor.

Len opened her eyes abruptly, rubbed at them with the back of her wrist, and murdered her lemur a little more.

"Where am I?" she asked.

"You're in the kitchen. In the new house. I think you're very sleepy. Let's go to bed."

"Sleep in your bed?" asked Len.

Noe looked out the blackness of the kitchen window. "Yeah. I guess so."

Len stared into the basement until Noe closed the door, "Werewolves down there," she said, as serious as an adult.

Noe took Len to her bedroom, pushed the mattress against the wall, and laid her sister down on it. She then dragged one of the metal pieces of the bedframe over until it lay on the floor beside the mattress. She made sure Len was cozy between her and the wall, which, judging by the fact that Len had already fallen asleep, she was, and then Noe tied her own wrist to the bedframe piece with one of her socks.

Warm, slow tears dripped down Noe's cheeks as she lay beside her sister. She stifled the sobs that threatened to push up through her throat and out her mouth. She didn't want to believe it. She had hoped it wouldn't happen to Len. But it had. Len was a sleepwalker. Just like Noe. And that was scarier than any basement.

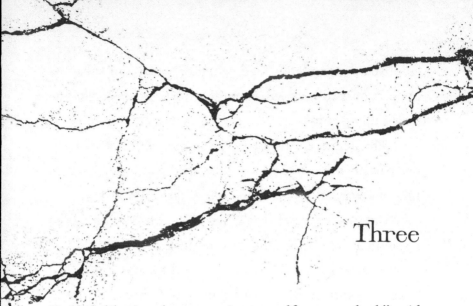

# Three

"I don't like it when you tie yourself to your bed," said Mom. She aimed a flathead screwdriver at a strip of bacon in a bubbly frying pan and harpooned it. She flipped the bacon onto a paper towel on the counter. She then hissed a duet with the frying pan as drops of scalding grease hit the back of her hand. "I also don't like that we can't find my tongs."

"They're here somewhere. We just need to get to the bottom of more boxes," said Dad. He was sitting at the kitchen table with Noe. Len was still asleep upstairs on Noe's mattress. Around them, boxes were stacked like a messy game of *Minecraft*.

"I don't like doing it either," said Noe.

"Noe, you haven't sleptwalked in weeks. I think you've grown out of it. The doctor said you would," said Mom.

"Isn't the past tense 'sleepwalked'?" Dad jumped at the opportunity to pick his phone off the kitchen table and start jabbing at it.

"The doctor also said it peaks at my age." Noe had told her parents the awful news. That Len was a sleepwalker. Like she was. And Noe didn't like their reaction at all.

"But you've been doing so well. And I don't even remember the last time you had night terrors."

"Parasomnia" was the doctor word for what Noe had. "Para" meant weird, like in paranormal. "Somnia" meant sleep. And that was it: weird sleep. Although it was worse than that. Much worse. Noe thought of it as dangerous sleep. Parasomnia wasn't a single condition. There were a dozen types of parasomnia. Noe was the lucky sufferer of two: sleepwalking and night terrors. She walked in her sleep. And sometimes she had vivid nightmares. It had all started about a year before, and it had been awful. And now her kid sister was about to go through it all too. And her parents were worried about tongs and past tenses.

"It *is* sleepwalked," said Dad softly, using the opportunity to check some other apps on his phone that had nothing to do with grammar.

"It doesn't matter about me, anyway," said Noe. "What about Len? Why aren't you worried about her? She's sleepwalking. You know how dangerous it is for me, and she's only three years old."

Mom laid a plate full of bacon on the table and sat down. "We've gone through this with you, and we'll go through it with Len. We're pros at it now. And it's a new place. Len might just be confused. That's all. Doesn't mean it's a long-term situation."

"Right," said Dad, grabbing a piece of bacon without looking up from his phone, and ripping off an end with his teeth. "I'm pretty sure I almost sleep-unpacked last night. Besides, the layout of this house is better for dealing with sleepwalking than our old house. Every outside door has a dead bolt, and both your and Nore's bedrooms are at one end of the hall. . . ."

"Stop it," said Mom.

"What?" asked Dad, looking up and widening his eyes in fake confusion, the strip of bacon dangling from his mouth.

"Her nickname isn't Nore. It's Len. We're not calling our kids Noe and Nore."

"Why not? It's clever and endearing."

"It's confusing and embarrassing. You're with me on this, right, Noe?" Mom pushed the plate of bacon closer to Noe.

"It's confusing and embarrassing," said Noe, picking at a piece of bacon but not lifting it from the plate. "We're not twins."

"Well, what I was saying," said Dad, "is that I can put

up *Len*'s old baby gate at that end of the hall. That'll keep her from wandering. You'll just have to remember not to crash into it when you go to the bathroom at night."

"That doesn't protect her from me," Noe said.

Mom slapped the table hard enough that the bacon jumped. So did Noe. So did Dad. The boxes surrounding them seemed like the only objects unaffected by Mom's sudden anger. "Don't say that," said Mom. "That thing with Abby was . . . just something that happened."

Abby had been Noe's best friend. One night, she'd had a sleepover at Abby's house. It was before Noe knew about the parasomnia. She had woken up surrounded by her parents and Abby's. Abby wasn't there. Noe's parents took her home and told her she'd attacked Abby in the night. They didn't go into details. They still wouldn't. But Abby had never talked to her again.

The worst part was that she didn't remember hurting Abby. She just remembered the night terror. A large purple snake was floating in the dark, coming right for her like it wanted to bite her head off. It moved stiffly, like it was half frozen, but when it got closer it start twisting and contorting faster and faster until she woke up. She'd had that exact same night terror a few times since. Even thinking about it in the daytime made her uncomfortable. But because of it, she had hurt Abby. Although it wasn't her fault.

"Even if Len has the same issues you did, it's different this time," said Mom. "And I mean more than the house. When you were dealing with it, it was only me and your father helping you. And we knew very little about parasomnia at the time."

"We only just now learned the past tense of sleepwalk," said Dad, grabbing another piece of bacon.

"Len has three people watching over her. Three people who are now experienced with the condition. So let's eat this screwdriver-flavored bacon before your father finishes it all, and get back to unpacking boxes. This house is a maze of cardboard."

The entire day was dedicated to boxes. Mom and Dad had taken the week off work for the move, and since it was summer, Noe had plenty of time to help out. Too much time. Even Len, once she woke up, tried to help. Her job was to stack the empty boxes by the back door to be flattened and shoved into the big green recycling bin, but mostly she drew windows and doors on the boxes and crawled inside them.

The entire week was like that. A slow limbo of brown cardboard and moving familiar items into unfamiliar places. Getting her room right. Not really caring about getting the rest of the house right until Dad or Mom raised their voices a few decibels. Every night she went to bed exhausted, and maybe because of that she didn't sleep-walk, although like Mom had said, it had been weeks since the last time it had happened. Len didn't sleepwalk again, either. All that work plus worrying over her little sister had pushed the warning from the girl with the stone around her neck right out of Noe's mind.

Until she saw the thing in the mailbox.

Noe had opted for staring out the front window instead of pulling one more thing out of one more box. The air from the plastic desk fan cooled the sweat on her arms and forehead. She realized she hadn't seen any activity outside the house all week, other than a car pulling out of a drive-way here or there. Instead of an R in the DEAD END sign, the vandal should have crossed out the END. That's what this street was. Dead Street. The kids she had seen on that first day acted more like zombies than kids. Why weren't they out riding bikes or playing basketball or lying in the middle of the road, like Dad had said?

Her eyes roved the street, looking for any activity. She'd even take a squirrel at this point. That was when she noticed something wedged into the flag of the mailbox.

That was enough of an excuse to take a break from unpacking.

Noe walked out the front door and marched down the slight slope of the front yard, past the two tall oak trees that she'd already decided would sport a giant spiderweb between them next Halloween. At the old house, three steps out her front door and she was in a busy street, and ten more steps and she was on the neighbor's front porch across the street. Here, twenty steps away from the front door and she was still in her own front yard, standing on grass spotted by yellow dandelions. She looked up, the oak trees towering above her and framing the sky in their branches. She'd heard once that a person's property extended up all the way to space, so maybe they owned that patch of sky just like they owned the trees and the dandelions and the grass.

The mailbox was big and black and metal with a rusty red flag. She was sure it wouldn't last a week. This was their first chance at a real mailbox, so Dad would probably replace it with something quirky and embarrassing like a barn with an open door or a fish with a giant mouth. Their old house had had a small, boring metal bin nailed to the house.

The thing stuck in the mailbox flag was an envelope. White and long like the kind her parents kept in the junk drawer but never used. She opened the box first, but it was empty. She pulled the envelope away from the flag. The paper was bendy, like there wasn't much inside, and there was no postage or address on it. On the side where the address should have been, written in large, shaky letters, was her name. Sort of. It was misspelled N-O-E-L. She opened the envelope.

Inside was a paper doll cut from gray construction paper. It had a round head and a rectangle body and long arms and legs. The edges were unevenly cut, like it had been done by a child with dull scissors. The body of the doll was blank, but its face had been drawn with crayon . . . and it was terrifying. Purple eyes that seemed too big and staring. Large red splotches on the face like it was bleeding. A red slash of smile that made her uncomfortable. A child's version of a monster. Horrifying. When she flipped it over, it had two letters in black crayon on the back, punctuated with oversized periods: S.M.

Noe looked around the neighborhood to see if the sender was spying on her, watching her open the strange delivery and hoping for a reaction. But the neighborhood was as still as it had been for days . . . until she saw the house at the tip of the dead end. The white one on the slope of the ravine. Something moved in an upper window, a slight shifting of a curtain.

Noe got angry.

She lifted the doll into the air and made a big motion of ripping it up while looking directly at that window. She was angry because she had gone down into that basement. By herself. After dark. Because there was supposed

26

to be something to be afraid of there. But there were worse things to be afraid of than pranks for the new kid on the block. Like falling down the stairs or wandering out in the streets or hurting somebody you care for without being able to help yourself and your little sister about to go through the same dangers and torments that you had to put up with and lose friends over and can't hide from because it could happen any night while you were asleep and helpless.

Noe dropped the pieces of the paper doll to the ground. She tried to run inside before the tears started. If it had been the front lawn of her old house, she would have made it.

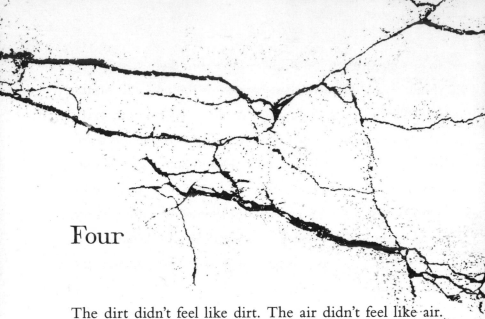

# Four

The dirt didn't feel like dirt. The air didn't feel like air. Noe couldn't tell if she was inside or outside, if it was day or night. Nothing around her felt familiar or right.

She was easing out of a sleepwalking episode. Time seemed to flow strangely, and she couldn't be sure if anything she heard or saw or felt was real. The dream world and the awake world didn't have hard lines. Elements of one blended into elements of the other. She just had to wait it out.

Noe didn't usually wake up in the middle of a sleepwalking episode. She often only knew she had sleepwalked if her parents told her the next morning. Sometimes they found her standing in front of an open fridge without moving. Or a turned-off television set. Or on the porch. Or screaming from a night terror in a corner. They would lead her back to her bed and tuck her in, where she would finish her sleep the way she was supposed to. The way most people slept.

But every once in a while she woke up in the middle of one of her sleepy ambles. It was confusing, and she had to spend minutes separating dream from real life, stacking up the evidence for or against in neat piles in her head like she was folding laundry, figuring out why she was standing in her pajamas in the garage in the dark or why she was sitting in Len's closet. It never got easier.

Noe stomped the floor with her bare feet to assure herself she wasn't dreaming. But it wasn't a floor. It was dirt. But it wasn't like dirt. It was hard. Like a floor. She touched a wall. But it felt rough and uneven and cracked like a cliff face. Not like a wall. She had touched the water heater, but that hadn't helped. It looked like metal, felt like metal, but the metal was warm.

Finally all the puzzle pieces floated slowly together like they were on the surface of a pool of water. She was in the basement of her new house. And she had sleepwalked. For the first time in her new house. For the first time in many weeks.

She hated this so much.

Noe found herself on the far side of the furnace and water heater, staring at the wall with the giant crack that traveled from ceiling to floor. She looked over at the windows, but they were solid black. She had no clue what time it was. Just that it was night. She stared in a daze at the wall, like she was sick with a stuffy head and couldn't focus. She stared harder at the wall. At the crack among the cracks. Focusing on the long jagged line that stretched the length of the wall in a diagonal path like it was a lifeline that would keep her firmly in reality.

And then, out of that crack, she saw movement.

At first Noe though it was water, not for any reason other than that her mind couldn't come up with anything else that would be seeping out of a crack in a stone wall.

"Seeping" was a good word. "Oozing" was better. It looked like toothpaste being slowly pushed out of a tube. Or like when Len was pushing Play-Doh through the holes in her cupcake factory play set.

She watched the movement for a few minutes, but for some reason couldn't bring herself to get closer to the wall to see what it was. She stuck near the water heater, her left hand trailing behind and touching its warm surface like it was home base in a game of tag.

Whatever was coming out of that crack was flat, more like one of those wide noodles from her mom's pasta maker than like toothpaste, although it was much wider than those noodles.

And then she noticed the flatness had a shape. A head

shape. A flat head like on a paper doll, but the size of a real head.

Noe thought of the gray paper doll she had ripped to shreds, the pieces of which probably still littered the base of the driveway.

She was hit with a wave of vertigo, like the dank basement air had thickened around her and was being stirred. Noe continued to stare at the shape extruding slowly out of that crack. It was about a foot or so out of the wall, sticking out into the air like a giant tongue.

She realized there was no sound. No slither or scrape of the thing as it slipped out of the wall, just a thick silence like there was no such thing as sound.

The flat form oozing from the crack in the wall bent up to reveal a face. A horrible, grayish face. A face that looked abused. Wounded. Smashed. Like a truck had run over it. Bruised and ripped with raw muscle and skull showing through, but all of it no more than a fraction of an inch thick. It had oily black hair and unearthly violet irises that shimmered in the gloominess of the basement like it had LEDs for eyeballs.

And it smiled. As it continued to slowly flow through the crack, it smiled at her.

That's when Noe felt trapped.

It felt like she wasn't watching of her own will anymore. Like the basement had constricted to an inch around her, not letting her leave. She knew this feeling, she realized. Just like she knew the feeling of slipping from sleepwalking into real life. She hadn't woken up. This was a night terror. You weren't supposed to remember your night terrors. But she always did. Every detail. And the worst thing about them was that she couldn't escape them. She endured them, and then she woke up when they let her wake up. A type of scared that she was well familiar with settled at the bottom of her stomach. A helpless scared. She hated that type of scared.

It felt like another ten minutes for the flattened creature to free its shoulders and elbows. Its arms were held at its sides, its hands still in the crack, as it wavered like a lazily rearing cobra. The upper body was strewn with grayish rags that were embedded into its flatness, and the whole thing floated parallel to the ground like a ribbon tied to the grille of a fan. Except for its face, which continued to bend up and gaze at her with those purple eyes and smile at her with that ripped mouth full of teeth. Any moment now its hands would be free. And then after that, its legs. And then it would be out of the crack. And who knows what would happen after that.

The staring, grinning creature slowly reached its newly freed arms toward her.

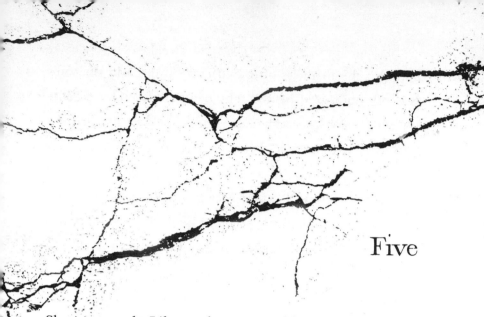

# Five

She screamed. Like a three-year-old. Like Len would have screamed. The scream seemed to shake her loose. Noe turned around and sped across the hard dirt without throwing another look back. She dashed up the stairs and burst into the kitchen.

"Mommy! Daddy! Mommy! Daddy!" She didn't see either one of them around, and the rooms were all dark, so she ran upstairs, ricocheting here and there against the boxes on the floor. The boxes felt real. She reached the stairs and ran up, her feet falling heavily on the carpeted steps. The steps felt real. They sounded real. It was completely quiet in the bedrooms, and the baby gate at the end of the hall was open. But she turned to the other side of the hall, to the open door of her parents' room.

"Mommy! Daddy!" Noe dived into the bed and felt her

body hit the firmness of unexpecting limbs and the soft-ness of unprepared bellies. The bed felt real. Her parents felt real. They lurched awake, Dad knocking the bedside lamp over with a crash of broken glass as he clumsily tried to find the switch on it.

"What's wrong?" asked Mom. "Night terrors?" The concern was immediately evident. Not just because of the violence of her entrance. Noe realized she had been calling them "Mommy" and "Daddy." She hadn't done that since first grade. The bright beam of a flashlight blinded her. Dad had pulled it from the bedside table. He didn't even try to hide the fact that he was only wearing boxers.

"There's something in the basement. A thing," said Noe breathlessly.

"Noe, are you awake?" asked Dad, shining the light into her eyes

"I'm awake," she said, squinting in the beam. "I think I'm awake. I'm not sleepwalking now, right? I'm not hav-ing night terrors?" She slowly made eye contact in the dimness with first Dad and then Mom. Measured actions. Purposeful movements. Controlled responses. The evi-dence of someone not asleep.

"You seem okay," said Dad.

"Why were you in the basement?" asked Mom.

"I was sleepwalking, and I woke up down there. But

that doesn't matter. Not this time. There's something in the basement."

"A mouse?" asked Dad.

"No, it's a . . ." She couldn't bring herself to say "a monster." She already felt like Len overreacting to bedtime. "No, not a mouse. Please come. Follow me."

Again feeling like a little child, she grabbed Dad's hand and towed him to the top of the stairs, Mom following close behind.

By the time she got to the basement door, she had stopped holding Dad's hand. Noe must have slammed the basement door shut in her flight. It loomed there like a guardian, not wanting her to pass. She didn't want to pass, either. The next moment was going to be a bad one. No matter what happened.

If that monster was there, she didn't know what she'd do. If he wasn't there, she still didn't know what she'd do. She wanted it to be there so that her parents could see it. She wanted it not to be there so she could convince herself that it hadn't been real. That she had imagined it. That it was a night terror. Or that this strange house in this strange neighborhood with its strange kids had conspired to trick her imagination into seeing it.

"You first," she told Dad, who hadn't had a chance to throw on a pair of pants or a robe. He looked extremely vulnerable, all soft and pale and round and hairy.

He went steadily down the stairs like he was going to switch over the clothes from the washer to the dryer. Noe followed, and then Mom.

At the bottom of the stairs, Dad looked around casually, the same way he would check under Len's bed and in her closet for werewolves. Noe did the same, but more like when Len herself would look under the bed or in her closet, scared and knowing with childlike certainty that something was there. The basement looked empty. Except for the washer and dryer. Except for the boxes. Except for the metal box of the furnace and the tall cylinder of the water heater.

"So where is it?" asked Dad.

"And what is it?" asked Mom, who had stopped at the halfway point of the stairs. She was in socks and didn't want them to get dirty. What kind of house was this that you had to wear shoes to go to the basement?

Noe didn't know how to answer. The flat monster didn't seem to be there. She peeked quickly around the water heater. Nothing. The crack was just a crack. She looked at the other cracks on the other walls. Nothing. The she felt her chest grow cold at a sudden realization.

A flat monster could hide anywhere.

Even in an open room like this. It could hide on the

other side of the water heater or slip under the washer and dryer . . . or slide behind the boxes.

"Was it a snake? Did it go behind the boxes?" Dad persisted when he saw her looking at them.

Noe approached the boxes like she was mesmerized by the brown cubes. There were six stacks of four boxes, each stack about five feet high and pushed together into a wall of cardboard. Yes, it could easily have slipped behind those boxes. Was probably watching her between the cracks in the stacks, its breath moistening the cardboard as it waited for her to get closer.

"Are you okay?" Dad asked again.

Noe leaned forward to peer between the boxes. "I think it's behind . . ."

Movement elsewhere caught her eye.

It was the same crack in the same wall. The large crack that traveled from the floor to the ceiling on the wall on the far side of the water heater. A movement somewhere in the middle of the crack, at a point where it ran parallel to the ground—the same movement she had previously misinterpreted as water gathering to drip down the wall, the same movement that she now recognized as a flattened head oozing its way through the crack, slowly, slowly, slowly . . .

"It's right there!" she screamed, covering her mouth

with one hand and pointing a finger at the monster. Mom ran down the steps, socks and all, to stand behind her, putting her hands on Noe's shoulders, and Dad spun quickly around to look where Noe's finger was pointing.

They all stared at the wall. At the giant crack.

The monster's head was only halfway out. Like it had rewound itself in the time she had run upstairs. It had started its exit from the crack all over again. Any second now, its head would bend up. She would see its purple eyes, its bruises, its bone, the wide grin on its grayish face as it looked directly at her. She whimpered.

"What are you pointing at, Noe?" Dad asked, his voice soft.

"That thing! In the crack!"

"Oh, in the crack?" Dad started walking toward the crack.

"Dad, stop." Noe grabbed at Dad's bare arm.

"Noe." He shook off her hand and walked to the crack. He stood close to the head of the monster, scrutinizing the wall as if he were planning out a mural for it. Meanwhile, the head kept creeping slowly out, like a letter in slow motion through a slot. Dad bent over to take a closer look at the crack itself, and the head started bending up. Their faces were about to be inches from each other. Noe closed her eyes tight. She didn't want to see what was about to happen.

"I don't see anything in the crack. Was it a centipede?" Dad asked. Noe opened her eyes again. Dad was staring directly into the purple eyes of the monster. "We've left the doors open a lot, moving stuff into the house. Who knows what kind of critters slipped in from the forest?" He stuck the tip of his index finger into the crack, right beside the head of the creature, right where its flat shoulder was about to emerge any second as it continued to seep from the wall.

"You don't see that . . . that thing? It's right beside you," said Noe.

Dad turned back to her. "Noe, there's nothing here but a crack in the wall. They're all over this basement. It's an old foundation. Nothing to worry about."

His eyes.

Dad's eyes.

They'd changed.

The irises weren't brown anymore. They were a pale violet. And shimmering. Like the monster's eyes. Noe sucked in her breath.

"I don't see anything either. Can you describe it?" asked Mom behind her, removing her hands from Noe's shoulders. Noe turned around. Mom's eyes, normally dark green, were the same terrifying hue as Dad's.

Noe stepped away from Mom, backing her way to the staircase. She spun, running up the stairs and out of the basement, and she didn't stop until she was in her own room, the door shut, her entire body buried in the blankets and pillows of her newly assembled bed.

Eventually she heard a door closing downstairs. Noises in the kitchen. Footfalls on the stairs. Down the hall. The click of the child gate. Her door opened, and her parents entered. Her purple-eyed parents.

"Noe, look at me," said Dad.

"I don't want to," said Noe in a voice muffled by blankets. She thought maybe the monster was with them, standing behind them, all three with matching eyes glowing in the darkness.

"Come on, Noe," said Mom. "We've been through this before. It'll feel better any minute now. You just need to calm down and fall asleep. Morning always fixes everything."

Finally they coaxed Noe out of the blankets. Dad had put on a white T-shirt and blue sweatpants. Mom had thrown on a maroon robe. Noe didn't see a flat monster with them. They had brought her some water and a peanut butter sandwich, the same stuff they always brought her during a bad sleep episode. Noe looked at their eyes. It was difficult to see in the dark. "Can you turn the lights on?" she asked.

Dad stood up and flicked the switch. Noe looked

straight at Mom. And then at Dad.

Their eyes were normal. A normal green and a normal brown.

Her parents eventually returned to their own bed. She could hear the plastic snap of the baby gate closing after they passed through it.

Noe pulled the covers up to her chin and stared at the ceiling. What was that thing in the basement? How did the neighborhood kids know about it? Why had it gone back into its crack the first time she had run away? Was it still in the crack? Had it followed her? That was an awful thought. She looked around her room. At the space under the door. The slats in her closet. The inch that her window was cracked open to relieve the heat. A flat monster could get through any of those spaces. It couldn't be kept out. It could be in the room right now, hiding behind her dresser or behind her headboard or under her bed.

Noe hid under the covers again and did math problems in her head. Her doctor had told her to do that when she was scared. If you do math problems, you'll eventually get more bored than scared, and then you'll fall sleep.

Noe did finally fall asleep, but on the side of the bed away from the thin space between her mattress and the wall.

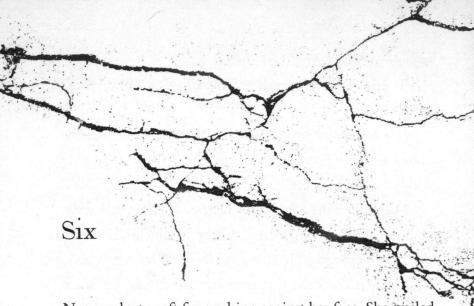

# Six

Noe awoke to soft fur pushing against her face. She smiled and reached out to pull the fur closer, awaiting the cold, twitching nose of the dog on her cheek. But then she smelled the awful aroma of banana and remembered that they didn't have a dog.

She snapped her eyes open and threw herself away from the edge of the bed, which should have landed her against the hard wall on the other side, but instead landed her against a soft mound of fur, like she was in bed with a giant beast.

Finally all her senses started working together and she realized she was surrounded by stuffed animals. More like buried in them—a menagerie of hellbenders and capybaras and okapis and bush babies and meerkats and all the other obscure and exotic animals that Len loved. Her little sister stood at the side of the bed, a half-peeled, half-rotten banana in one hand and a plush wallaby that was supposed to be the next animal in the plush cocoon she was making for Noe in the other.

"What in the world are you doing, Len?"

"Protecting you from werewolves," Len said around a disgusting mouthful of soft banana.

And then Noe remembered. The sleepwalking. The basement. The flat monster. Her parents' eyes. She jumped out of bed in an explosion of fuzzy chinchillas and echidnas and blob fish and kakapos and started throwing on clothes.

"Where are you going?" asked Len.

"Don't worry about it. Just keep playing with your animals." Noe grabbed her phone, noted that it was almost ten a.m., and dashed downstairs. Her parents were elbow-deep in boxes. She tossed out an "I'm going outside. Be right back!" at them and then darted behind a stack of boxes and out the front door before they could reply.

The temperatures were shifting from morning cool to afternoon muggy. The grass was dry, and the blue sky was so blank, it was like a giant reflector for the heat of the sun. She tried to remember which directions those creepy kids had gone on that first day. Any of them. But she had only a vague memory of them moving away from the house.

Then she remembered the movement in the window

of the white house at the tip of the dead end when she had found the paper doll.

She walked around the arc of asphalt toward it. The house was relatively isolated at the end of the street, as if nobody wanted to build on either side of it. On one side of the house, a thin dirt path wended up the gentle slope and disappeared over the top of the hill.

From afar, the white house seemed like every other house on the block, old-fashioned and very New England. But the closer she got, the more she realized how really old it looked, in the negative sense. It looked uncared for. Abandoned, even. The white siding was dingy and cracked. The red paint on the door and window shutters was speckled and peeling. The grass on the small front lawn looked as wild as the forest surrounding the property. She didn't see a mailbox.

Strangest of all, somebody had painted a large black X on the dirty white siding beside the red front door. It looked freshly painted and seemed to sparkle like the R on the Dead End sign at the opposite end of the neighborhood.

The X reminded her of something Mom had told her when they went hiking once. Noe had pointed out a group of trees with orange X's on them, and Mom had told her they were marked to be removed. When Noe asked her why anybody would want to remove trees, Mom guessed that the trees were diseased or infested with bugs and needed to be taken down before they fell on a hiker or infected the trees around them. Whatever the reason, it was so the tree removers would know exactly which trees to remove and which trees to leave alone.

Noe stared at the shimmering black X and the dilapidated house it was painted on. The house did seem diseased, and she couldn't imagine who would be living here. She was about to find out, though.

She crossed the lawn and ascended the cracked concrete steps to the front door. There was a doorbell to the side, but after pressing it a few times, she decided it didn't work and banged hard on the wood with her knuckles.

Nobody answered. She knocked again. Maybe this place was abandoned. But then who had been looking at her out that window? She looked up at the window and saw curtains covering it.

Eventually, Noe walked away from the house. She was relieved that nobody had answered. That she had been saved an awkward confrontation. But then she thought of Len sleepwalking down into the basement and that thing in the crack. She had to try another house.

There were about a dozen houses on the block, and there were three kids standing at the edge of her lawn on the day she moved in. If she had to knock on the door of every house in the neighborhood to find one of those kids, she would.

She continued around the curve of the dead end to the next house, which was blue and shaped like a barn. It was the house almost directly across the street from her house. It had a white door with no X beside it. This house was staying. She rang the doorbell.

A woman opened the door almost before Noe had pulled her finger back. The woman was wearing black yoga pants and a loose green T-shirt and had beads in her hair like the girl with the stone around her neck. Noe suddenly realized that this was not like her at all, walking up to strangers' houses and talking to adults she'd never met so that she could talk to kids she'd never met. Her face flushed as the woman waited for her to speak.

"Hello," said the woman. "I think you moved into the house across the street, didn't you? The red house?"

"Yes." And then she heard Mom's voice in her ear. She corrected herself, "Yes, ma'am. I'm Noelle Wiley."

"Noelle? As in French for Christmas?"

"Yes."

"How nice. I love Christmas. I'm Mrs. Harris." The conversation paused. Neither was sure where to take the conversation after a Christmas reference in the summer.

Finally the woman said, "How can I help you, Miss Christmas?"

"I'm looking for kids. Somebody my age. Do you have any . . . Is there . . ." It was a ridiculous request. She was phrasing it like she needed to borrow a garden tool.

The woman didn't look at her like she was making a ridiculous request. She broke into a large smile. "Oh, I think I've got somebody for you." She turned into the house and shouted, "Radiah! You've got a visitor! Radiah!" Mrs. Harris stopped and then looked back at Noe. "She's probably all the way up in the attic. She's always up in that attic. I'll ding her."

Noe had no idea how to ding a person, but she followed Mrs. Harris down a hallway lined with framed family photos and black-and-white sketches of landscapes into a kitchen full of appliances and decorations from another decade. Mrs. Harris hit a button taped above a wall-mounted phone with a corkscrew cord and raised buttons. It was hanging from the yellow-papered wall beside a green refrigerator. Nothing happened.

Mrs. Harris sensed Noe's confusion. "It dings in the attic. That way, we don't have to shout for her. We just press this button, and me and my husband get an instant daughter."

They stood together in the kitchen for a length of time

that seemed much longer than an instant and long enough to get awkward. Eventually a girl sidled into the kitchen, although that didn't make it less awkward.

It was the girl with the rock around her neck. She was still wearing it. The girl didn't say anything. She stood there looking down, like she was in trouble. Or like she was very interested in the tips of her shoes.

"There's somebody here to see you, Radiah," said Mrs. Harris.

The girl named Radiah slowly raised her head. Her eyes widened briefly, but that was the only way she acknowledged Noe.

"This is Noelle Wiley. Her family moved in across the street. Into Erica's old house." Radiah seemed to slump farther down, like she'd suddenly lost a couple of vertebrae. Mrs. Harris turned to Noe. "Radiah can be shy." She turned back to her daughter. "Her name's Noelle. Like Christmas. That's pretty, right?"

Radiah nodded her head slightly.

"You can call me Noe," said Noe.

"Oh, that's not as pretty," Mrs. Harris said.

Radiah nodded her head slightly again.

"Why don't you take Miss Christmas out to the backyard? Or better yet, show her some of the trails in the forest. You need to get out of that attic."

"I'll show her my room," Radiah said.

Mrs. Harris sighed. "Okay. But play a game or something. Smile. Be happy."

"Yes, ma'am," said Radiah, walking toward the stairs. Noe followed.

The stairs topped out at another hallway. More black-and-white sketches were framed on these walls, this time of horses and cows and other barnyard animals. They passed a few bedrooms with pristinely made beds and spotless floors and well-arranged bookshelves.

"Do you have any brothers or sisters?" Noe asked. The family photos she'd seen downstairs only had Radiah and her mom and dad in them, but the question worked to fill the uncomfortable silence.

"No," said Radiah without turning around.

"Which of these bedrooms is yours?"

"None of them." Radiah stopped in front of one at the end of the hall. She shrugged her shoulders. "Well, this one used to be mine." Noe peeked in and saw another room that seemed to have never known an occupant. The walls were green and the comforter on the carefully made bed matched them. A desk against one wall had pencils and paper on it, perfectly laid out like a desk at a furniture store. A couple of crayon drawings that looked like a kindergartner had done them were taped to the walls. "But it's not far enough away."

Against what she'd just said, Radiah entered the

immaculate room. Noe followed her. But instead of sitting on the bed or turning around to talk, Radiah walked across the room to the closet door. She opened it and entered. Noe heard the creak of boards.

Noe approached the door and realized it wasn't a closet. A set of stairs rose up into darkness. She heard a click, and then the area above went from dark to dim. A thin metal chain above the top stair danced below a bare, burning bulb. Noe walked up the stairs.

It was a bedroom. In an attic. But like the bedroom of somebody who had snuck into the house and nobody knew they were sleeping there. The room had no ceiling. The walls angled to a point and were made of bare wooden beams. A small, dirty window facing the neighborhood let in a minimum of light. The floor was also bare wood, with here-and-there tufts of yellow insulation poking out. An old rug had been thrown down on the wood, along with a brass bed, a rocking chair, and a dresser. The dresser had more of those black-and-white sketches scattered across its top. All around the makeshift bedroom were dusty boxes and chests and old furniture. It was like Radiah had pushed everything to the edge and made her own space. Before Noe could ask her why she stayed in the attic when there were so many bedrooms, she noticed a piece of paper taped to the dresser. A gray piece of construction paper that had been cut into the shape of a monster.

"You put that thing in my mailbox?" asked Noe.

"What?" said Radiah, who still hadn't looked Noe in the eye. Instead, she looked where Noe was pointing. "Ruthy" was all she said. Radiah walked to the dresser, balled up the paper monster, and threw it as far as she could into the attic, where it disappeared into the clutter and darkness.

"I ripped mine to pieces," said Noe. Radiah didn't reply. She just kept staring into the part of the attic where the ball of paper had disappeared.

Noe didn't know what to do with this girl. It was like she was one of the boxes back in her own house, taped shut in two different directions, with the word FRAGILE scrawled across it. But she guessed she didn't really need to do anything with the girl. She just needed to find out what was in her basement.

"I saw it," Noe said, gazing into the dusky edges of the attic space.

Radiah didn't acknowledge the statement.

"That thing you just threw away. I saw the real thing. Coming out of the wall in my basement. It was . . . awful."

Radiah continued to ignore her, instead focusing on a cloud of dust motes floating in the light from the hanging bulb. She stuck her hand in the cloud, and watched the

51

glowing points scatter like tiny fish in water.

"What's in my basement?" asked Noe. But Radiah continued to focus on catching dust in the light.

"Why won't you answer me?" Noe was getting angry. She could feel warmth suffuse her chest and arms and face. Her voice had a slight tremor to it, and her hands shook. If this girl didn't answer her, she . . . she didn't know what she'd do. Yell so loud the girl's mother would come up here. Push over furniture. Grab the girl by the arms and shake her. Whatever she needed to do to get answers.

Radiah finally looked at her. It was a flat gaze, emotionless. It made Noe uncomfortable. "I warned you not to go down there."

"What is that thing?" asked Noe.

"You don't want to know. Just stay away from the basement, and you'll never need to know."

"How am I going to live in a house and never go in the basement? That doesn't make sense."

"I don't go in my basement. Just don't go in yours."

"This is ridiculous. There is something in my basement, something terrifying, and you know what it is, but you're not telling me. Are you a jerk? I don't understand. You and your friends come to my house to give me warnings. You slip things in my mailbox. But you won't explain. If this is a game to mess around with the new girl on the street, it's

52

not fun. I need to know what's down there, not just for me, but for my little sister."

"We're trying to help you."

"What is that thing in my basement?" Noe's voice quivered in anger.

Radiah sighed and looked at the tips of her shoes. "The Smashed Man."

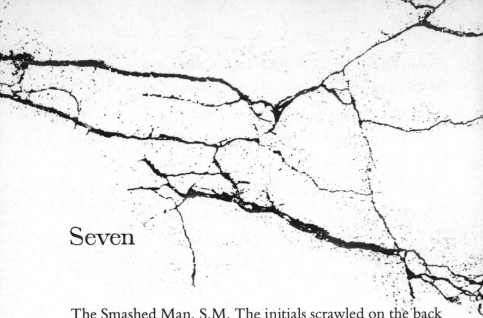

# Seven

The Smashed Man. S.M. The initials scrawled on the back of the paper doll at her mailbox. Noe stared at Radiah, waiting for more, but Radiah had stopped, like those two words were the only explanation she had. Finally, without looking up at Noe, she said, "We should get the rest of the Dread Enders together for this."

"Just tell me what he is."

"I don't know what he is."

"What do you know about him?"

"Nothing."

Noe threw her arms in the air. "You know enough to warn me that he was down there! You know enough to leave a paper doll of him in my mailbox! It was awful. The way he looked at me as he came out of the crack . . ."

Radiah jumped up off the bed. "You didn't let him come all the way out, did you?"

Noe shrugged her shoulders. "I didn't let him do anything. I ran away. Why is he in my basement?"

"He's in all our basements," said Radiah, her eyes dropping to the floor and her bottom back to the bed.

"What do you mean?"

"What I said. He's in all our basements. Every house on Dread End. At least, every house with kids in it." She looked away into the forest. "That's why I stay in the attic. To get as far away from him as I can." Radiah shook her head, the beads in her hair softly clacking. "This is too much for me to tell you by myself. I need the rest of the Dread Enders. We should go to Rune Rock."

Noe threw her arms in the air again. "Who are the Dread Enders? What is Rune Rock? Why aren't you making any sense? Should I even be talking to you? What kind of crazy neighborhood did I move to? We shouldn't have done this. The house wasn't *that* good of a deal."

Radiah quietly ignored the barrage of questions while she tapped on her phone. It had a custom case with an image like the sketches downstairs—tall, dark pine trees on a white background. But suddenly Radiah slammed the phone down on the dresser so hard the case cracked, a jagged black line cutting through the trees. She didn't seem to care. She was suddenly a streak of fire. "You're right. You shouldn't be here. Erica should. Erica should be okay and with us and not in a coma somewhere in Texas. A coma that got you that 'good deal.' She should still be in her house. Not you. Not your family."

Radiah left her cracked phone on the dresser and stormed down the stairs. Noe stood for a second, shocked, confused, embarrassed. But she had no choice but to follow. All the way to the front door. And then to the house next door.

This house was black and looked like a witch's house. Like it shouldn't be in a neighborhood in the United States but planted by itself in a clearing in a forest somewhere in Europe. Noe briefly considered returning to her own house across the street, but she couldn't let this go. Not with the Smashed Man in her basement. She didn't like knowing his name.

The door to the house was wide open. Radiah shook her head. "Mr. Larson always forgets to close the door. It's dangerous. Anybody could walk right in." She walked right in.

"Wait . . . shouldn't you ring the doorbell?" asked Noe.

"Ruthy's like my kid sister. And it's just her and her dad here, and he lets me come over any time. Not that it's any of your business." Noe thought she liked the quiet version of Radiah better than the angry version.

Radiah shouted, "Ruthy!" and started walking up the stairs to the second floor. Noe followed uncertainly.

"I'm up here!" The voice came down the stairs like a

ghost, small and weak.

Radiah stopped halfway down the hall and walked into a room. Not once did she look back to make sure Noe was still there.

Noe stopped two steps into the room. Everything was covered in paper monsters.

An unending chain of paper dolls had been looped around the room. They were all made of gray construction paper and taped to walls, stacked on dressers, spread out on the floor. Tiny, horrible faces scrawled in red and purple crayon leered at her from every direction.

"I hate these," said Radiah to the little girl on the floor. Ruthy looked about six years old. She was playing with crayons and paper, exactly what Noe would have expected a child her age to be doing in her room. Except she would also have expected her to be making animals and Disney characters. Not the Smashed Man over and over again. Radiah ripped down a paper monster taped to the bed and dropped it to the floor. She sat on Ruthy's bed and grabbed a large plush penguin that was lying there, put it on her lap, and rested her chin on its head. "Ruthy thinks that if she keeps making these paper dolls, the Smashed Man won't come into her room."

The little girl on the floor winced at the name of the monster.

Noe knelt down beside Ruthy. "Hi, Ruthy. I'm Noe."

"I know. That's short for Noelle. Did you get the thing I put in your mailbox?" She gestured with her scissors to the paper monsters surrounding them all.

"That was from you?"

Ruthy nodded.

"It scared me."

Ruthy looked down at the piece of gray construction paper in her hands. She was cutting a Smashed Man out of it. Only its head and shoulders were free, like the way Noe had seen the real Smashed Man. "I wanted to warn you better. Don't go into your basement at night."

"She already did," said Radiah. "She didn't listen and now she's one of us."

"One of us?" asked Noe.

Radiah sighed. "We'll tell you everything. There's not much, but we'll tell you. But we need to wait for Crystal."

"Who's Crystal?"

"She's the other kid on this block," said Radiah.

"I'll check to see if she's walking over," said Ruthy, jumping up and leaving the Smashed Man unfinished at her feet. She crossed the room to look out her bedroom window. "She's here."

Ruthy and Radiah immediately left the room. Noe walked over to the window. A girl was standing on the front lawn. She had long brown hair and a long summer dress and seemed really tall. She wasn't looking around. Wasn't checking her phone. Wasn't doing anything but waiting. A few seconds later, Noe saw Radiah and Ruthy come out and meet her. They didn't hug or smile or greet each other. They stood there like they had stood at the edge of Noe's front yard. Like they were afraid of the houses, the street, the air. And then they all looked at her. Radiah lifted her hands, palms up, in an impatient gesture, and Noe realized she was alone in somebody else's house. She hurried outside.

# Eight

The three girls stared at Noe as she exited Ruthy's house. Noe didn't know why they were wary of her. She wasn't trying to be their friend or force her way into their group. She just had questions. Besides, they had made first contact. The phrase made her think of herself as a space explorer landing on an alien world.

"Quickest way into Old Man Woods is through your backyard," said Radiah.

"What's Old Man Woods?" asked Noe.

"The forest on the edge of the neighborhood," said Crystal. "I'm Crystal."

"Noelle." Crystal was also wearing a rock around her neck and, Noe now realized, so was Ruthy. All were smooth stones with large holes in them, strung through with a rough leather cord. "Why is it called Old Man Woods?"

"You'll see," said Radiah. "Can we cut through your yard or not?"

"Sure," said Noe.

Radiah headed across the asphalt toward Noe's house. The other two followed like they were on their way to detention.

Noe fell in step behind Ruthy. "Why are we going to the woods?" asked Noe.

"That's where Rune Rock is," said Ruthy.

"What's Rune Rock?"

"It's a rock with this on it." The girl drew a symbol in the air with her finger that Noe didn't catch. "We hang out there a lot. There's no basement under Rune Rock."

"You don't have to answer her questions, Ruthy," said Radiah. "She'll see everything when we get there. And then we can figure out what to do with this situation." Noe wasn't sure if "this situation" meant the monster in the basement or Noe herself.

"Let her talk. She's fine," said Crystal. Radiah turned her head just enough to give Crystal the side-eye.

Ruthy shrugged and stuck a thumb over her shoulder toward the abandoned house. "That's the path to the school." She was talking about the line of dirt that wended beside the white house and over the lip of the ravine. "The school parking lot is over the top."

"It must be awesome being so close to the school. I've always had to take the bus."

"I don't start there until September. I'll be in first grade then. But Radiah walks it. And so did—" Ruthy stopped and started again. "Radiah walks it, but Crystal doesn't. She doesn't go to school."

"Doesn't go to school?"

Radiah spoke from her lead position without turning around. "In winter, the plows pile the snow from the school parking lot at the top of the path. It's like a ten-foot-tall ice mountain."

"What do you do then?"

"Either slip our way over it, walk the long way around, or get our parents to drive us. The other option is to stay warm at home and let your mom teach you."

"Shut up, Radiah," said Crystal.

Noe couldn't tell if they were being mean or that was just how they were. They both spoke in the same flat tone of voice. Either way, there was a definite tension in this group, and Noe felt uncomfortable being around them.

The group crossed Noe's front lawn and walked past the side of the house. At head level was the kitchen window. Noe looked through it and could see the black door to the basement. She caught Radiah looking at it too, but Radiah quickly averted her eyes when she saw Noe looking at her.

They walked the edge of her backyard, past the large firepit. "Is your family going to host the summer bonfire?" asked Ruthy.

"I don't know what that is," said Noe.

"The neighborhood has a bonfire every season," said Crystal. "Since we're surrounded by trees, we get a lot of falling leaves and limbs. And every big storm seems to take an entire tree down. We make bonfires to clear all that out. It's also an excuse for a block party."

"I like the winter bonfires the best. All the Christmas lights and hot chocolate," said Ruthy.

"It gets dark earlier in the winter," said Radiah.

They walked until the soft grass of the backyard gave way to the crunchy leaves of the forest floor. Noe saw trees painted with red arrows, marking the path.

"You'll get lots of animals in your yard from the forest," said Ruthy, turning to Noe and almost smiling.

"What kind of animals?" Noe asked.

"Foxes and turkeys and deer and fishers. Sometimes coyotes. My dad said that one time a moose came out of the forest and walked down the street."

"What's a fisher?" asked Noe.

"It's like a giant, scary weasel. Some people call them fisher cats, but they're not cats," said Ruthy. Noe wondered if Len knew about fishers.

The path hugged the bottom wall of the ravine. From down here, Noe couldn't see any of the houses atop it. Only the cliff going straight up. They continued through the break in the ravine wall until the path crossed a stream at a short wooden bridge. Radiah ignored a red arrow on a tree that clearly wanted her to continue on the path and instead followed the stream into the brush. The rest followed without hesitation.

"This is why it's called Old Man Woods," said Radiah, slapping the white bark of a birch tree as she passed.

Noe looked around the forest and saw the dark greens and browns shot through here and there with the shocking white tree trunks, like the dark forest was hair and the birch trees were streaks of white in it.

About five minutes later, the four girls and the stream arrived at a copse of birch trees, their bark gleaming bright in the summer sunlight. In the middle of the copse and about a dozen feet away from the stream was a boulder the size of her family's SUV. The entire forest was littered with boulders. There was one about half this size on the edge of the yard behind her house that Len had already christened Wombat Rock for no good reason. The kid would fit right in with the rest of these Dread Enders, giving boulders weird names.

Except that, unlike Wombat Rock, this boulder *was*

weird. Painted on its face was a large deformed R in sparkly black paint, like the one on the Dead End sign. "Another R?" said Noe.

"What?" asked Radiah, who was clambering up the lichen-covered boulder. Crystal sat cross-legged on a patch of emerald moss, and Ruthy settled onto a fallen tree with large disks of orange shelf fungus rising from its bark. It felt like a court room, with Radiah as judge, Crystal and Ruthy as jury, and Noe as the accused.

"Like the one on the Dead End sign," said Noe.

Radiah kicked her heels against the rock and gazed down at the rune between her shoes. "The runes."

"What are they?" asked Noe.

"Nobody knows," said Crystal.

"They've been here as long as the rest of us," said Radiah.

"How long have you all lived here?"

"All my life," said Radiah. "So has Ruthy. Crystal was three when she moved here."

"I don't remember living anywhere else." Crystal threw a rock into the stream. It made a soft *blurp*, which was followed by a splash as a frog interpreted the falling rock as a threat and dived into the stream.

"And we're the only kids on the block?"

"Now that Erica's gone," said Radiah.

"And Brett doesn't count anymore," said Crystal, poking a finger in the soft moss.

"Brett?" asked Noe.

"My older brother. He's in college out in California."

"And your little sister," piped up Ruthy, who was holding a stick topped by a shiny green beetle, swinging it slowly around like a magic wand. "What's her name?"

"Lenore." Noe looked around at the three girls. None of them was looking at her. "So what happened to Erica?"

"Wait a second," Radiah said loudly from her judge's bench. "We've let you ask enough questions. It's our turn. When did you see the Smashed Man?" The other two girls glanced down at the ground when they heard the question.

"Last night," said Noe. It felt weird telling strangers about what she still thought of as a private nightmare. What happened in the basement didn't feel real at this second, standing in the middle of a forest with a bunch of weird kids.

"I told you not to go down into your basement at night," said Radiah.

"And I told you that was like telling her to go directly into her basement," said Crystal. "What happened?" she asked Noe, and the ridiculous image of a forest trial came to her again.

66

"The first time, nothing."

"What?" asked Ruthy, and Noe could almost feel the hope radiating off her.

"You're lying," said Radiah.

"Don't call her a liar," said Crystal. She looked at Noe. "But . . . are you sure it was nighttime?"

"It was almost midnight. I was probably down there for fifteen minutes. Nothing." She left out the part about Len sleepwalking.

"That's weird," said Crystal.

"Everything about this is weird," said Noe.

"But last night you did see it," said Radiah, the judge prodding the witness to clarify her testimony.

"Yes. After I got your paper doll." Noe nodded at Ruthy, who looked at her tight-lipped, her hope dashed. "I tried again. And I saw . . . something . . . coming out of a wall in my basement. He looked like that paper doll, completely flat like he had been rolled out on a cookie sheet, but the size and shape of a person. He had a . . . a messed-up face. It was terrifying." She left out the part about her sleepwalking.

"He didn't get out, did he?" asked Crystal. She looked at Noe as if her answer was the most important thing in the world.

"He got almost halfway out, I guess, before I ran away.

I got my parents and went back down. He was there again, but he had started over. Like he had been sucked back into the crack while I was gone. But my parents . . ."

"Purple eyed," said Ruthy. "Like the Smashed Man."

"And they couldn't see him." Noe was starting to get worked up. "What was that thing? What happened to my parents?"

"Okay," said Radiah. "If you're going to be one of us, you should know everything. At least, everything we know."

"I didn't say I wanted to be one of you," said Noe.

"It's not up to you," said Radiah. "As long as you live on Dread End. As long as you live above the Smashed Man. As long as every day is a bad one because you know there's a monster in your basement that no adult can protect you from . . . whether you like it or not, you're one of us."

"None of us like it," said Crystal.

"I just need an explanation," said Noe.

"Can't give you that," said Radiah, leaning forward on the rock. "Like I said, we call him the Smashed Man. And we have no idea who he is. We don't know where he comes from. He's just always there. Anytime you go into the basement at night, he's there, oozing out of the cracks, staring at us like he wants to eat us alive or rip us apart."

"And he's in all our houses?" Noe asked, remembering what Radiah had said in the attic.

"Yes," said Crystal.

"Why?" asked Noe.

"Nobody knows," said Crystal.

"What happens if he comes all the way out?" asked Noe.

"We don't want to find out," said Radiah.

"Why can't our parents see him?"

"No adult can see him," said Crystal. "Their eyes turn that weird shimmery violet color, and they act like nothing's there. It's almost worse than the Smashed Man himself."

Noe found herself agreeing with Crystal. She would never forget her parents' eyes in that basement. "What have you found online?" she asked.

"There's nothing about it on the internet," said Radiah.

Noe cocked her head to the side and squinted her eyes. "Everything's on the internet."

"Look for yourself," said Radiah.

"I will."

"You won't find anything. You just have to live with it. Like us. And it sucks."

"I hate it," said Crystal. "Hate it. Hate it. Hate it. We stay out of the basement as much as we can, and never go down at night, but knowing he's always down there, waiting for us . . . I hate it."

"Why doesn't he just come out?" asked Noe.

"We don't know. And we don't know why he only tries at night. And when we're there. We don't know why he starts over every time. We don't know why adults can't see it," said Radiah. "We don't know anything."

Noe thought for a moment and remembered the black-and-white werewolf movie she had shown Len. "Every monster has rules," she said.

"What?" asked Crystal.

"Every monster has rules. Werewolves need a full moon. Vampires need blood. What are the rules of . . . the thing in our basements?" She hadn't said the monster's name out loud yet. She wasn't ready. That would make him too much a part of her life. She didn't want him to be any part of her life.

"Those are stories," said Radiah, shaking her head in disgust. "We're talking about real life at Dread End."

"Erica might have seen him come all the way out," said Ruthy.

"*Now* can I ask who Erica is?" asked Noe.

"She lived in your house before you," said Radiah, looking down at the rune. Bugs flew around her head, but she didn't bother to swat at them. "She was found in the basement of her house. Your house. In a coma. Her parents had to take her to a special hospital far away."

"Texas," said Ruthy.

"Texas," Radiah continued. "They had to leave fast. That's why they sold the house so cheap." Radiah said it like it was the fault of Noe's family that their friend had fallen into a coma and was moved away.

"You think he got her?" Noe asked.

"I don't know what happened. Erica had gotten secretive. She was up to something," said Radiah.

"Erica was always up to something," said Crystal.

Radiah nodded. "Erica always talked about the Smashed Man differently than we did. She'd only lived here three years. Was always trying to figure out a way to beat him."

"She attacked him once," said Crystal.

"No way," said Noe.

"Yeah, with a softball bat. We were there. She tried to crush his head before his arms came out of the wall. But when that bat hit him . . ." Crystal shivered.

"There was a flash of light, like she had attacked something made of electricity," said Radiah. "It knocked her backward. There were scorch marks on the bat."

"Whatever happened the last time, she probably wanted to protect us by keeping us out of it," said Crystal.

"Lot of good that did," said Radiah loudly. "Now we're worse off. She's not around, and now the Smashed Man has two more victims in her house."

"I miss Erica," said Ruthy.

"We all do," said Crystal, getting up and trudging through the dead leaves to wrap her arms around the little girl. "Even if some of us have a hard time showing it."

Radiah rolled her eyes and swatted hard at a bug in the hot air.

Noe wanted to go home. Away from these strange kids with their strange stories. She wanted to board up the basement door. She didn't care if they never washed another shirt again. This was awful. Absolutely awful. She wished she had never seen that ad for the house.

The Dread Enders grew silent again—they were really good at that—and after a few moments, without speaking or looking at each other, they got up and followed the stream back to the path until they reached Noe's backyard. Noe led the way once they got there. As they walked around the side of the house to the front lawn, she could see the abandoned house around the curve of the dead end. She looked at the sparkly black X on it in the same sparkly paint as the Rs on the Dead End sign and Rune Rock. She decided to ask them about the house. "Hey . . . ," she said, turning to face the other girls. She didn't finish the sentence.

All three girls had shimmery purple irises.

The Smashed Man had gotten out. And judging by the direction their purple eyes were looking, he was right behind her.

Noe screamed and ran into her house.

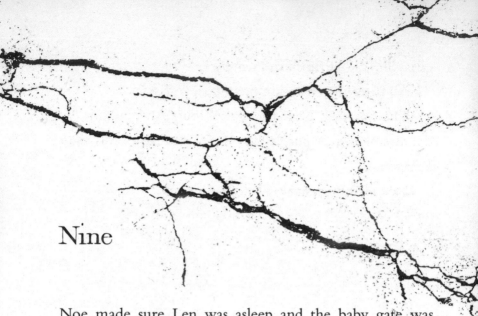

# Nine

Noe made sure Len was asleep and the baby gate was latched, and then got into bed with her laptop. She could hear a low, sporadic mumble of conversation from her parents down the hall in their room, but otherwise the house seemed to be shutting its shades for the night. Everywhere except for in the basement, that is, where a monster was spring-loaded in a crack in the wall, waiting for Noe or Len to set foot on hard-packed dirt.

Noe opened the laptop and went to Google. She searched for every variation of the phrase "Smashed Man." She tried Flat Man. She tried Flat Monster. She tried Thin Man. Thin Monster. Flat thing in my wall. Nothing. Nothing relevant, at least. She tried all the creepypasta sites she knew. She tried to find any books about the subject. She couldn't believe that something was not mentioned on the internet.

And then she thought of her parents' purple eyes and wondered who could write about something that they couldn't see. And then she thought of the Dread Enders' purple eyes.

After she had screamed and run inside earlier that day, she immediately looked out the window, afraid that she would see the Smashed Man wrapping its flat arms around one of the girls. Instead, she didn't see any sign of the Smashed Man. Just the girls filing slowly and calmly to their houses. They hadn't even followed her to her house to see why she had panicked. It was like the way they treated the Smashed Man. No curiosity, no action, just suffocating under a weight of powerlessness and inevitability.

After Noe had calmed down, she realized that she was more confused than scared. Those girls could see the Smashed Man. They would have run if they had seen him. And why did their eyes change color? They weren't adults. They also said that he only came out at night. And that he had never gotten out of their basements. Nothing made sense.

Still, she didn't leave the house the rest of the day.

Noe googled Totter Court, but that didn't help. Just some real-estate information sites. The same on the socials. The same kind of information that had pulled them to this house in the first place.

Finally she gave up, shutting her laptop and putting

it on the desk. She grabbed a black scrunchie out of the drawer and tied her right hand to the bedpost.

She almost didn't need to. She barely slept. She couldn't stop thinking about what was two floors below, waiting for her to come down and set him free. It was maddening. The Smashed Man in her basement. In everybody's basement on Totter Court. And nobody knew what he was. Was he a ghost? She could deal with ghosts. Ghosts move furniture and make weird noises, but they don't do much else in the stories. But a Smashed Man. A Smashed Man. Something that she had never heard of. That not even the internet had heard of.

But he had rules. Every monster had rules. She knew some of them already. He only came out at night. He restarted every time you left. And he made people go purple eyed. Just adults, the other girls had said, but Noe had seen them their irises go violet too, so that was a rule that needed to be figured out. But those were rules. And if he acted according to rules, he could be defeated by rules. Like werewolves and silver. And vampires and stakes through the heart.

She eventually fell asleep and dreamed she was in an old movie, running through a shadowy castle and looking for a flat coffin where a monster slept.

Noe spent a good bit of the next day unpacking and

organizing and cleaning. She couldn't believe her family had this much stuff. It felt like more than the house could hold. She was putting some of Mom's books on a shelf when she had an idea. She ran upstairs to her room, opened her laptop, and called up the website of Osshua's local paper. The site was archaic and amateurishly designed and a minefield of broken URLs, so it took her a while to find what she was after. Or, more accurately, to find out that what she was after wasn't online. She had hoped that the newspaper archives had been digitized. But they weren't. They were housed at the library.

"Mom!" she yelled.

"What?" Mom yelled back from somewhere downstairs.

"How far away is the library from us now?"

"What?" said Mom.

"The library!"

"Just come down here!" said Mom. Noe reluctantly unfolded herself from the laptop. Downstairs, she found Mom scrubbing out the cabinets in the kitchen. Mom couldn't put dishes and food in these strange cabinets without cleaning them first with her own hands, even though the people who sold the house had had it professionally cleaned.

"How far away is the library from us now?" asked Noe.

"It's about the same, I guess. You want to go? I could use a break from cleaning. And I'm sure Len could use a break from . . . whatever she's doing."

A knocking on the front door interrupted Noe's answer. A soft knocking. Like whoever was doing it didn't actually want anybody to open the door.

Noe thought for a second about letting whoever it was have their wish, but then went ahead and opened the door. It was Crystal. She was wearing another long dress and her long hair was done up in a bun on top of her head, making her look even taller. She was staring at her hands, which held a yellow notebook in front of her like a tray. Crystal looked up, startled that somebody had answered her knock, and Noe was relieved to see that her eyes were blue instead of purple. Crystal didn't say anything. Just looked back at the notebook. The voice that ended the silence was neither girl's.

"Who's this, Noe? Are you going to introduce me?" Mom walked to the door, her hand holding Len's as Len jumped up and down like she was testing gravity.

"This is Crystal. She lives in the neighborhood."

"Hi," said Crystal.

"Good to meet you, Crystal." Mom looked at both girls. "So are we still going to the library?"

"I need a banana!" screamed Len as if she had just

realized that bananas were a thing.

"All right. Calm down. I'll get you one." Mom led Len into the kitchen, leaving Noe and Crystal facing each other across the doorway like reflections in a mirror.

"You won't find anything about the Smashed Man at the library," said Crystal, still staring at her notebook. "We've all looked. The internet, the library, the newspaper archives. Erica even tracked down some adults who grew up here. They didn't remember the Smashed Man."

"Why are you here?" asked Noe.

"Why did you run away yesterday?"

Mom returned, leading Len, who was already two bites into the leopard-spotted banana in her hand.

"I changed my mind on the library. Is it okay if I just hang with Crystal?" Noe asked.

Mom turned her head in the direction of the kitchen, where her cleaning supplies littered the countertops and floor like a closet had exploded. "Sure." She turned to Len. "You still want to go to the library, honey?"

"Yes!" shouted Len, holding up her banana like a sword.

"You two have fun," Mom said to Noe and Crystal as she scooted Len out the door. As Len passed, the little girl stared at the older girls with intense eyes, slowly chewing a mouthful of soft yellow like she distrusted them together.

After the door shut, Noe said, "Mom's really going to hear it when they get five minutes down the road and Len realizes she forgot to bring one of her stuffed animals. She's obsessed with stuffed animals. The weirder the animal, the better." Crystal nodded at the information. "You want to see my room?" asked Noe.

Crystal paused for a moment, blowing air into her cheeks before replying, "I kind of want to see your basement."

"My basement?"

"I haven't been down there since before . . . whatever happened to Erica . . . happened."

Noe didn't want to go into the basement even in the daytime, so she just stood there, paralyzed, while Crystal fiddled with the leather cord at her neck, the stone at the end hidden under her blouse.

"Those rocks you guys wear," said Noe. "What are they?"

"Witch stones," said Crystal, pulling hers out and holding it so that Noe could get a good look. "They're for protection. Erica told us about them. You find them in streams, smoothed and with a hole worn through by the water. They're rare. It took us forever to find three in the stream out in Old Man Woods." She stuffed it back into her dress. "We never found a fourth one for Erica."

"Do they work?" asked Noe.

"Nah," said Crystal. "It's kind of stupid. But what else can we do? We've tried crucifixes and hamsas and sage. It gives us something to do. It's better than nothing." She looked around what she could see of Noe's house. "The basement?"

Noe led Crystal to the black door in the kitchen. After opening it and flicking on the light switch, they both gazed down into the monster's lair/laundry room.

"Are you sure you want to go down there?" asked Noe.

"Yes." Crystal took off down the steps. When they both hit dirt, Crystal turned to Noe and said, "Of all the basements I've seen on Dread End, yours is the spookiest."

"Thanks," said Noe, looking around at the stone walls and dirt floor. Her eyes were pulled to the parts of the large crack that she could see on the other side of the water heater. She couldn't make herself believe that the Smashed Man wasn't coming through any second.

"They found her here on the floor, in a coma," said Crystal.

"What happened?"

"Nobody knows." Crystal looked over at the nook with the washer and dryer in it. "Erica was braver than the rest of us. Once we learned nobody could help us, not our parents, not the internet, not any other adults, we gave up. Just dealt with the fact that a monster in our basement would . . . do something . . . to us if we ever stayed too long down there at night. Erica, though, she thought we could beat it."

"How?"

"I don't think she knew. It was just a hope. She used to read a lot, on top of the dryer right there."

"What? Here?"

"Yeah, she said she liked the noise of the machines while she read. She'd run them even without clothes inside. She only did that in the daytime, but I have no idea how she even did that. My days in my basement are torture."

"Why do you spend your days in your basement?"

Crystal paused again, playing with the corner of the yellow notebook. "I'm homeschooled."

That explained the comments from Ruthy and Radiah during the walk to Rune Rock. There was a time after the incident with Abby that Noe had wished that she was homeschooled. That she didn't have to show up where everybody was talking about her. "What does that have to do with your basement?"

"My mom thinks that having a part of the house dedicated to just school helps us—or just me now, I guess—focus."

"Oh no." Noe looked at her in horror.

"Yeah. My schoolroom is the basement," said Crystal. Noe didn't like being in this basement for the five minutes they'd been in it, but to have to go down every day, for hours a day, seemed like torment. "I have to look at the crack in the plaster every day. Or try not to look at it. It makes me crazy. I fake sick a lot. One time I tried to cover all the cracks with putty. It didn't work."

"Does it always come through the same crack?" Noe cast a worried look at the large crack on the far wall.

"Seems to." Crystal had been looking at the dryer the whole time they had been talking. Finally she turned to Noe and asked, "Why did you run screaming from us?"

Noe had almost forgotten. She took two steps back from Crystal. "Your eyes. They turned purple. All three of you. Like my parents' eyes did. Like . . . his eyes." She glanced over at the crack.

Crystal raised her hand to her mouth, her own eyes darting to the crack. "Are you sure?" The question was muffled through her fingers.

"Yeah. I turned around, and . . . I thought it meant that the Smashed Man was there." His name. She had said his name. Not ten feet from the crack, she had said his name.

Crystal chewed her lip. "That is what it means. But it doesn't happen to kids. And as far as we know, he's still in the basement walls." She shrugged. "We didn't see anything after you left and nothing happened to us, so maybe your own eyes tricked you."

Noe was pretty sure about what she had seen but decided not to push it.

"Erica did that once," said Crystal.

"Did what?"

"Screamed and ran away from us." Crystal looked down at the notebook in her hands. "It happened in Radiah's front yard. She told us afterward that she spooked herself. Kind of happens in this neighborhood."

"What's the notebook for?" asked Noe, looking for any excuse to stop talking about the Smashed Man. And purple eyes.

"It's my book about the Smashed Man."

*Great,* thought Noe. "Your book?"

"There's no record of the Smashed Man anywhere. Not that we can find. So I started my own record. There's not much in it, but I thought you'd like to see it." She held it out tentatively, like she was afraid Noe would dash it from her hands.

Noe took it from her and flipped through at random. It was all words, no pictures. There were descriptions of the Smashed Man. Descriptions of each basement and the cracks that he came through. Descriptions of the Dread Enders themselves.

One page at the end was a numbered list. The same list

that Noe had gone over in her head last night. Above the list was the phrase *Every Monster Has Rules*.

"I added that page last night because of what you said at Rune Rock," said Crystal.

Noe didn't know if Crystal expected her to read the whole thing in front of her, so she continued to flip through the notebook. But then she hit a page that she did read completely. One that was marked with a bookmark made of gray paper shaped like a man. The page was a poem written in careful letters.

What can the Smashed Man do?
He's flat. Must be easy to escape.
Run upstairs.
But the Smashed Man can slither up a staircase
Like a snake.

What can the Smashed Man do?
He's flat. Must be weak.
Run to your bedroom and shut the door.
But the Smashed Man can squeeze underneath the door
Like smoke in a house fire.

What can the Smashed Man do?
He's flat. Must be slow.
Stay out of reach in your room.

But the Smashed Man can slip behind your headboard
Like a shadow.

What can the Smashed Man do?
He's flat. Must be powerless.
Dive into bed and cover your head.
But the Smashed Man can smother you in your sleep
Like a deadly, grinning blanket.

That's exactly what the Smashed Man can do.

Noe closed the notebook and stared at the yellow cover until Crystal took it out of her hands like it had been a mistake to show her. "I should probably go," Crystal said. "Thanks for showing me your basement." She went upstairs, and Noe heard the front door open and shut.

Noe didn't like being in the basement, and certainly not alone, but all she could think about was Erica sitting on that dryer, reading.

Noe walked over to the big white machine. Who was this girl who had lived here before her? Who had been so fearless despite living above this monster? It felt like Noe was taking her place. In her house. With her friends. She wondered if she had even taken her bedroom. They did have one major difference . . . Noe was the opposite of fearless.

Noe climbed up on the dryer and sat down, her legs dangling over the front. The metal was hard and uncomfortable, but it did give her a good view of the giant crack across the room.

Then something caught her eye between the dryer and the wall. It looked like a book had fallen down and gotten wedged in there.

She crammed her hand into the crevice and, after spending a few seconds trying to get her fingers on it, finally pulled it out, scratching the cover and her knuckles on the rough rock wall. It was bound in mint-green cloth and had a gold sun on the cover. Not a book. A diary.

Noe opened it to the inside cover. There, in the upper left-hand corner in sparkly black letters, it read:

Erica Bays
Age: 13
6 Totter Court, Osshua, NH

Noe turned to the first page. On it were only two lines of text.

To Radiah, Crystal, and Ruthy:
If you are reading this, the Smashed Man got me.

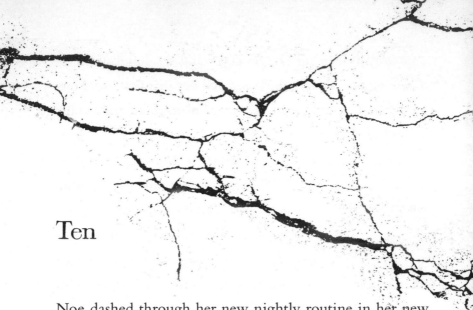

# Ten

Noe dashed through her new nightly routine in her new house. First, check on Len. Make sure she was tucked in bed. Next, check the baby gate. Make sure it was fastened to the wall and the door clicked shut. After that, slip into her own bed. Normally, she would then open her laptop and search the internet for any clues about the Smashed Man before reaching for the black scrunchie she hid under her pillow to tie her wrist to the bedframe. Every morning, she woke with a dead arm and had to get through the excruciating pain of all the blood rushing back into it. The sensation was like a thousand needles being jammed into her arm, but it was worth it. The scrunchie was almost comforting. She needed that wrist manacle as much as she needed a pillow to fall asleep.

However, this time she shut her door, which she usually

left open in case Len started sleepwalking. Then, instead of pulling out her laptop, she pulled out Erica's diary. Noe had wanted to sit down and read it from the moment she had found it. But Dad had returned home moments after Crystal left, and when he learned that Mom and Len were at the library, he decided he and Noe should go out and meet them to have dinner. Noe had hidden the diary under her pillow with her scrunchie until bedtime.

Noe leaned against the headboard and opened the diary to that strange introduction: "If you are reading this, the Smashed Man got me." She was about to turn the page when the sound of her door opening almost made her throw the book across the room. Dad stood there, punching away at his phone, like he needed GPS directions to find his own bedroom. It was too late to hide the book under her pillow, so she just let it drop to her lap, like it was any other book she would read before bed.

"You're supposed to knock," said Noe.

"Sorry," said Dad, lifting his nonphone hand and rapping on the wall beside the door. "You seemed distracted at the restaurant, and I wanted to make sure nothing was wrong." He continued to look at his phone for a few more seconds before looking up at her. His eyebrows lowered as he saw the book in her lap.

Noe tried to distract him. "Is there a key to the

basement door?" She'd been thinking about that question since she'd first seen the Smashed Man.

Dad tilted his head. "You know what? I don't think so. But we don't need one. It's got one of those old-fashioned keyholes shaped like a chess pawn. There's no way we could accidentally lock it."

"What if we wanted to lock it? Can we put a padlock on it?"

"A padlock? Why in the world would we do that?"

"I'm afraid Len might fall down the stairs when she sleepwalks." Noe couldn't tell him the real reason.

"I don't think Mom would let me. An ugly old padlock right in the kitchen? Besides, that would make it really hard to do the laundry."

"What about one of those small sliding bolts, like hotel rooms have?"

Dad shook his head. "Too dangerous. What if somebody got locked in down there?" Noe actually shivered at the thought. That *was* too dangerous. "Besides, Noe, Nore will be fine."

"Len," Noe said automatically.

"Are you worried about yourself sleepwalking? Is that what this is about?"

"No," she said. "I'm worried about Len." That was true, at least.

Dad nodded his head and sat down at the foot of her bed. "Well, how about this . . . I mean, it's just a thought I had, but maybe if I say it out loud it will motivate me to get it done. I was thinking about turning the basement into a playroom for you and Len. Throw down a floor, throw up a ceiling, cover the walls and paint them, add some more light down there. You could have a couch, a TV, video games, anything you wanted. We'd never bother you down there. Except to do laundry, of course."

"What?" The word came out high-pitched and shrill. She immediately thought of Crystal and her homeschool room. She drew the blanket up close to her chin. "I don't want to play in a basement."

"It won't feel like a basement. It will feel more like your own private apartment."

"I don't want my own private apartment."

Dad laughed. "We'll see. What are you reading?"

The question was so abrupt, Noe didn't know how to answer it. She stuttered and managed a garbled "I don't know" before Dad picked up the book off her lap. He looked at it for a few seconds, turned a few pages, and then looked back at her.

Noe gasped.

Dad's eyes were an iridescent purple.

She jerked back from her father, hitting her head on the

headboard with a skull thud and kicking out with her foot, knocking the diary out of Dad's hands and onto the floor.

Then she realized that if Dad's eyes were purple, the threat was actually in the direction he was looking. Behind her.

The image of the Smashed Man rising behind her headboard, like in Crystal's poem, shot through her rattled brain. She screamed and threw her body away from the headboard and into Dad's arms.

But there was nothing there. No mutilated face leering at her from over the top of the headboard. She quickly scanned the room and saw no sign of the Smashed Man. Instead, she saw the slats in her closet door. The big dresser against the wall. Her own bed, which had a good twelve inches of space under it. All places that a flat monster could hide.

"Noe, what's the matter?"

Noe looked up at Dad, who was holding her with both arms like he was afraid she'd disappear. His eyes had returned to their default brown. "I'm sorry," said Noe. "I don't know why . . . I startled myself somehow . . . I don't know. I think I just remembered one of my night terrors."

The concern in Dad's eyes was as obvious as the purple had been. "What was it?"

She moved over on the bed and waved the question

away. "Nothing. It doesn't feel scary now. Stupid actually."

Dad looked at her for a moment before finally saying, "Okay. But, sorry, I thought it was just a book. I didn't realize it was a diary. I shouldn't have looked at it. At least you hadn't started writing in it yet. A brand-new diary for a brand-new house. I like that. One of my regrets is that I never kept a diary when I was growing up. I miss that kid." He stood up from the bed and picked the diary off the floor. He handed it to her and walked to the door, placing his hand on the doorknob. "Open or shut?"

Noe looked at the open doorway and then at the space under the door itself. "Doesn't matter," she said.

He nodded and left it open. "Please don't tie yourself to your bed tonight?" Noe didn't promise anything. Just cozied up in bed.

As soon as she heard the click of the baby gate, Noe opened the diary. It wasn't blank. Almost every page was filled with words and sketches. Why had Dad said it was new? She looked around the room again. No Smashed Man sliding out of a crevice to attack her. So why had Dad's eyes gone purple? She flipped to the beginning of the diary.

> This is a diary of my attempts to beat S.M.
> I hope it has a happy ending.

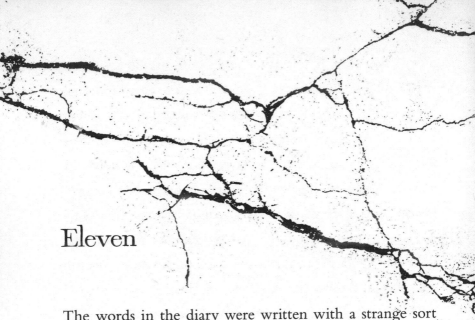

# Eleven

The words in the diary were written with a strange sort of ink, thick and black and shimmery, like what the runes were painted in. But portions were unreadable, the ink congealing into a solid mass in places. The ink in those congealed sections was tinted purple, although it still sparkled. Noe settled deeper into her bed and continued reading what was legible.

I've written it in star stuff so that the adults can't read it and think I'm crazy. I bought a fountain pen online and

The rest of the paragraph was a mass of purple ink. Star stuff? Was that why Dad had thought the diary was blank? And why his eyes went purple? She flipped to the next readable section.

Try Number One

PLAN: Have to start somewhere. Going to try the metal softball bat Mom and Dad keep under their bed (in case somebody breaks in, I think). Simple plans work best.

RESULTS: I hit him in the head with the bat. Didn't work. Felt like I shattered my arm and almost burned my hands off. The bat was scorched

I know you guys didn't like that I tried, so I'm not telling you about my plans anymore. Safer for you that way.

Noe flipped the page. Try Number Two was completely unreadable except for the title, and she couldn't see where Try Number Three or Try Number Four started or ended. Try Number Five was mostly intact, although portions had congealed into purple.

Try Number Five

PLAN: Brute force doesn't work. Sharp things don't work. Going after his eyes didn't work. Any time I touch him with something, I get bruised or burned . . .

water, bleach

soda, hair spray, milk

gasoline

RESULTS: Liquids roll off him like he's wax
makes the dirt floor wet, smells up the basement.

The next page just had one sentence on it:

I'm running out of ideas.

The pages after that were covered in shimmery purple blobs instead of shimmery black letters, so Noe wasn't sure what attempt number it was when she finally found a page that she could read. But what she read made her eyelids stretch.

realized none of you could see the white house. Your eyes went purple, like adults looking at S.M. Remember me screaming and running away?

Noe stopped reading and looked around like she was hoping to find someone sitting in the room to discuss this with. The words were confusing, and she wished the beginning of the page was readable, but it seemed like Erica was saying that the girls couldn't see the white house? Was that why their eyes turned purple? Not because the Smashed Man was out . . .

Noe thought back to where everyone had been standing when she saw their eyes go purple. They had been behind her, facing the white house. An invisible house. That couldn't be possible, could it? A house only Noe could see? And Erica. That somehow made Noe feel less alone. Even though she was still very alone, since Erica was comatose in a hospital bed half the country away. Noe kept reading.

> thought S.M. had escaped, so I went to the basement that night to see. He came out of the crack like always. I then had this horrible idea that there might be other monsters around Dread End like S.M. making your eyes go purple

> learned no adults could see it either. Looks like an ordinary house, except it has a large X painted on it in star stuff

What followed looked like a partial drawing of a house that had fused together with some of the text and turned purple. Noe picked up reading at the next legible part.

> I didn't tell you because you hate when I talk about S.M. too much. I know you'd rather we just live with it until we're old enough that we forget about it or can move away like Brett

seemed abandoned, so I broke in. Rock through the window. I don't think it counts as vandalism if the house doesn't exist to most people

That's when the snake in my dreams changed.

Noe let the book fall back onto her lap. The snake in her dreams? Noe's imagination conjured the purple snake she kept seeing in her nightmares. The eyeless one that floated in blackness like it was suspended underwater. The one that moved toward her slowly and then started twisting the closer it got. She picked the diary back up.

found a notebook full of symbols

On the next page, Erica had drawn the R from Rune Rock and the Dead End sign. Beneath the symbol was the word "Amberonk." Below that was a note that read, "For protection." Beside the R was an X. It was called "Nonatuke," and its explanation was "For hiding."

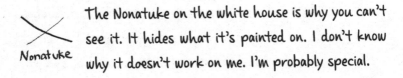

The Nonatuke on the white house is why you can't see it. It hides what it's painted on. I don't know why it doesn't work on me. I'm probably special.

Nonatuke

Erica had drawn a smiley face with its tongue sticking

out at the end of that last sentence. Noe had already started to like this girl who was courageous enough to hit a monster with a softball bat, but the joke made Noe like Erica all the way.

I don't understand the R's, the Amberonks. Who or what's being protected, and from who or what?

more symbols, but none of the others had explanations, only names

my snake nightmare. It's black and glittery and doesn't have eyes. It's fast and rushes at me until it stops, like it hits a wall. It twists like it's being bent by an invisible force. That's when I always wake up. That part's more terrifying than the snake.

Noe's forehead wrinkled as she read that paragraph. That wasn't her snake nightmare. Her snake was purple and moved slowly. But it was close.

The night I got back from the white house, I had the nightmare again. Except I didn't wake up when the snake started twisting. It bent into one of the sigils in the book: Elberex.

Here Erika had sketched three lines. The first was a simple horizontal line. Below that was another horizontal line, but with one end curving up and the other end curving down. Below that second line was a third one where the ends kept curving up and down until they touched in the middle of the line, creating a sideways eight. Noe recognized it as the symbol for infinity, but Erica had labeled it "Elberex."

no explanation for what the Elberex does, but I think it can destroy S.M.

Elberex

Noe read that part three times to make sure she had read it correctly. Erica thought she'd found a way to destroy the Smashed Man. With just a symbol. It was unbelievable. But so was the Smashed Man, and so were invisible houses. Noe turned the page and almost threw the book to the floor. It was the face of the Smashed Man, sketched in horrid detail.

Noe's arm skin goose-bumped as she imagined Erica sitting on the dryer in the basement with this diary in her hands, watching the Smashed Man oozing out, sketching until he was almost out, before running upstairs to reset him. She wouldn't have done that, would she? Willingly waited for the Smashed Man? Maybe. This was a girl who

100

took a softball bat to his head, after all. The only difference between the Smashed Man's face on the page and the Smashed Man's face in Noe's memory was that this one had the Elberex on its forehead.

need to draw the Elberex on S.M.'s head. I don't know how I know. Just do. Deep down. When I sit quietly with my eyes closed, I know it. Like I know my name and my parents' faces and the color of grass. But it wasn't just the symbol. I needed star stuff from the white house to draw it with and I need him to come out of the wall as far as possible, because I think that weakens him

More congealed ink. The inevitably of where this story was going shook Noe. She wanted to scream at Erica not to go forward with her plan. She wanted to slam the book shut. Wedge it back into the space between the dryer and the wall in the basement. To pretend she had never found it. She wanted to throw her blanket over her head. Beg her parents to move again. Run away. But she forced herself to keep reading.

know it's risky. I don't want any of you hurt. If it works, then I'll tell you right away and I'll burn this diary at the next bonfire really wish I had a witch stone right now. I really wish you guys could wish me luck. The only thing that has made life on Dread End bearable is all of you.

RESULTS:

That's where it ended. No result. None that Erica knew, anyway. Some of the pages at the end of the book were full of doodles, some congealed and others not. There were drawings of the Elberex—probably where Erica had been practicing—and lots of sketches of the Smashed Man. His face. His face with the Elberex on his forehead. Him coming out of a wall. The crack at the far end of the basement. Noe now knew that Erica had in fact sat there on the dryer watching the Smashed Man ooze out of the crack for many nights. Not so she could draw him. But to gather the courage she needed to face him. With glitter paint as her only weapon.

Noe put the book down, tied her wrist to the bedpost, and settled in to try to sleep. But all she could think about was what had happened two floors below. She wondered how Erica could have such confidence in such a strange plan. Painting a symbol on the Smashed Man's head? She wondered at what point Erica had realized her plan wasn't going to work. She wondered what the Smashed Man had done to Erica. She wondered what she should do with the diary and the white house and everything that Erica had kept from her friends. She thought about the eyeless snake. Then she thought about the Smashed Man, not down in the basement, but under her bed. Or under her mattress. Behind her dresser. Behind her headboard. She quickly untied herself, grabbed a pillow and blanket, and went to sleep on the floor of Len's room.

The only light in Len's room was the decapitated unicorn lamp beside her bed. It cast just enough illumination to show Len's face in the dark. Usually that's what it showed. This time it showed a fluffy toy civet staring at her from the hollow in the pillow where Len's head should have been.

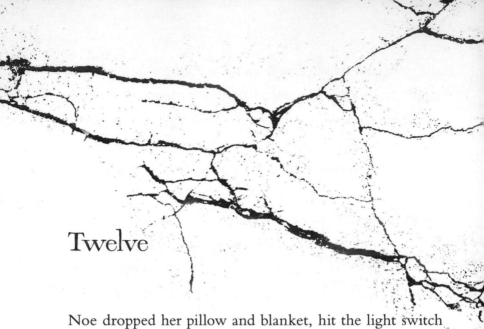

# Twelve

Noe dropped her pillow and blanket, hit the light switch in Len's room, and ran to the bed. She pushed around the bedclothes and stuffed animals. No Len.

She dashed back into the hall. When she saw that the baby gate was ajar, Noe's insides went prickly. She pushed through it and ran to peek into the darkness of her parents' room. She could hear Dad snoring. See vague, dark lumps in the bed. She couldn't tell if Len was one of those lumps. She stared at the spot where Len would most likely be and then flashed the light switch on and immediately off, too fast to wake her parents and too fast to see what she was looking at. She concentrated on the afterimage in her head. Mom lying on her side on top of the blanket. Dad on his back with a leg hanging out and his mouth open. No Len. Noe ran downstairs.

She was getting better at navigating the house in the dark, and she skidded through the living room and into the kitchen without turning on any lights. She could feel her heartbeat pulsing in every part of her body. Could feel wetness down her back that had nothing to do with the summer heat.

Even with the lights out, she could sense that the door to the basement was wide open. That the blackness of a void had replaced the blackness of the painted wood. Why wouldn't Dad just put a lock on this door? She could feel the square of night in the window behind her, like it was oozing a flood of tarry blackness to push her into that void.

But she didn't need the motivation.

Noe hit the light and tore down the stairs. At the half-way point, her socked feet slipped on the steps and her legs went out from under her. She grabbed the railing in panic and saved herself a fall down the stairs to hard dirt, although she hit her tailbone on the edge of a step, sending a painful shock up her back. She took a big breath, and then pulled herself to her feet and descended the last few steps, her legs a little wobbly. She didn't bother to look around once she hit the floor, instead racing around the water heater to the far side of the basement to the crack where the Smashed Man lived. She stifled a scream with her fist.

Len was there, her yellow pajamas strange against the

105

dirt floor and rock walls. Tiny in the dim space. A stuffed narwhal under one arm. A stuffed cassowary under the other. She wasn't moving.

The Smashed Man was also there.

He was slinking out of the crack. Almost all the way out of the crack. Wavering and floating in the otherworldly silence and the underground dimness like a nightmare. He was free to the middle of his thighs. His face was grinning and wild. His purple eyes so wide she could see the tops and bottoms of his eyeballs. The skin that showed through the rips and holes in his gray clothes was torn and wounded like his face. Whiteness that must have been bone shone through the red here and there. His extended arms were almost brushing Len's face. Len stood there mesmerized, like she was watching a movie that was too old for her. Not reacting. Not hugging her stuffed animals. Just watching the Smashed Man.

Except that she wasn't watching. Her eyes were closed. She was in a sleep state. Len had sleepwalked down here.

"Len!" Noe screamed, rushing to her sister's side. She grabbed Len's arm with one hand and, without thinking about it, swatted at one of the flat hands of the Smashed Man with her other.

Instantly she felt a shock ten times as bad as her bruised tailbone. She flew across the basement, taking Len with her. They barely missed the water heater. Noe felt her body hit the ground hard, the air knocked out of her, the basement swimming around her, blackness creeping at the edges of her vision.

She couldn't black out. Not with Len and the Smashed Man in the basement together.

Noe heard sobs and saw the stuffed animals sitting against the wall, dirty from having rolled to that spot. She got slowly onto all fours, and then leaned back until she was in a kneeling position. Finally she stood. Her entire body felt like the Smashed Man looked. Broken and bruised.

Len was three feet away, lying on her back like she was about to make a snow angel, her face wrinkled and wet from sniffling. Noe picked her up by her armpits and raced across the basement and up the stairs. The last thing she saw of the Smashed Man was him floating there in the air, only his feet in the wall.

Only his feet in the wall.

They crossed the line from wooden step to the vinyl floor. Noe shut the door and collapsed onto the kitchen floor with Len in her arms.

Only his feet were stuck in the wall. It must have taken a good five minutes for him to make that much progress from when she had first seen him. She gasped. She must have lost consciousness when she hit the floor. Her mind conjured a bird's-eye view of the basement five minutes before. Her lying on her stomach on the floor, motionless. The two stuffed animals against the wall. Len lying on her back, confused and hurt and crying. And the Smashed Man. Wavering on the air with his arms out in front of him, inching out slowly but steadily in their direction.

"Turn the light on!" said Len in a panic. Noe reluctantly heaved her body off the floor, every part of her aching, and found the light switch. The kitchen still looked gloomy with the light on.

Len was looking around and wiping her face. "Narrie. Cappie. Where are they?"

"Are you hurt?" Noe asked, kneeling beside her and looking at her face and hands. Light scuff marks on the back of one hand and on her elbows were the only visible signs that she'd been thrown across a room.

"Narrie. Cappie," Len insisted, pulling her hand away from Noe and wiping her nose with her pajama sleeve.

"Can you stand up for me?" asked Noe. The way Len was moving and the fact that she wasn't crying anymore were good news, but Noe wanted to make sure. If Len felt ten percent as bad as Noe did, Noe would need to tell Mom and Dad. And she had no idea what to tell Mom and Dad.

Len got quickly to her feet and asked about her stuffed

narwhal and cassowary again.

"They're still in the basement. We'll get them tomorrow."

"The werewolves will get them down there."

"I know. The werewolves. That's why we have to wait until morning."

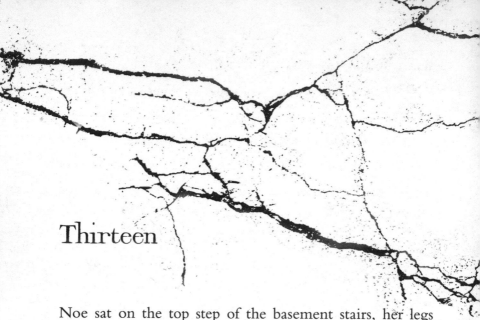

# Thirteen

Noe sat on the top step of the basement stairs, her legs stretched in front of her to rest against the steps below. The morning light glowed through the kitchen window in shafts sliced by the forest trees. She was eating a hard-boiled egg and a piece of buttered toast off a plate teetering on her knees. Dad had made them for her before heading upstairs to his home office. Mom was off to her office in Boston. Len was still asleep in Noe's bed.

Beside Noe were three objects: a diary, a stuffed fish with a unicorn horn, and a stuffed bird that looked like an ostrich with a bone sticking out of its head.

She gazed down into the basement and imagined it as a deep pool cooling her legs. Above the surface was one reality, below it another. Maybe that pool was an ocean, dark and mysterious, hiding scary things below the surface that could at any moment bite her legs off. Hiding one scary thing, really.

She felt herself turn ghostly.

That was how the rest of the Dread Enders must feel. Ghostly. That was what had shocked her about them when she first saw them. Even now that she had gotten to know them. They didn't laugh and fool around and play games and say stupid things. They were exhausted. Exhausted by terror. Exhausted by living their lives with the constant knowledge that below their feet was a monster. Exhausted by not knowing anything about him and not being able to do anything about him and being so isolated in dealing with him.

A part of her wanted to do the only thing that was within her control. To head downstairs one night and stare at the crack until the Smashed Man came all the way out. She didn't know what would happen, but maybe it was better than this, better to get caught by the Smashed Man than to live above his constant, low-burning presence, spooling and unspooling every time she went down into the basement, her parents literally blind to the danger. That was a decision the Dread Enders faced every day too.

"The werewolves didn't get them!" came an excited voice behind her.

Len stood in the kitchen with a stuffed ocelot under her

arm. She looked rumpled from sleep, and the scrape on the back of her hand was pink. She immediately tried to pick up the narwhal and the cassowary but dropped the ocelot. Then she tried to pick up the ocelot but dropped the narwhal. Finally she lined all three on the floor in a row and sat beside them. Then she stole the half-eaten piece of toast off Noe's plate and snickered as she took a large bite.

"There's no werewolves down here. They're in your closet, remember?" said Noe. The joke was out of habit. Len's eyes got big and she half stood up, like she was about to run.

"No, I'm sorry. I didn't mean that," said Noe. "There are no werewolves in your closet."

Len sat back down and pulled her stuffed animals close to her. She took another bite of toast, smearing butter between the corner of her lips and her right ear. "They're in the basement?"

Noe flicked her eyes over the dirt and stone at the base of the steps and weighed exactly what she should tell her kid sister. It might be a good idea to scare her away from the basement. But if she was sleepwalking there, that didn't matter, and scaring her would just make her little sister's awake life hard. "No, there's nothing down there but boxes and dirt. The werewolves are far away in the woods somewhere."

Len looked in fear at the window above the sink, which framed a section of the forest surrounding the house. *Oops,* Noe thought. She would have to think up a new faraway place to put Len's monsters.

"Come here," said Noe, placing the plate on the floor with a clink and pulling Len onto her lap. She wrapped her arms around her little sister and Len wrapped her arms around the ocelot and all three looked like a set of nesting dolls. Len was Noe's antidote to being too much of a Dread Ender.

"Do you remember last night?" Noe asked.

"Mom sang 'Silent Night' to me before bed." Mom always sang Len Christmas songs before bed. It didn't matter what time of year it was. And Len couldn't quite handle the word "silent" yet.

"Anything else?"

Len shook her head fast, her blond air weaving a wild halo in the air. She wiped butter off her face with the back of her scraped hand. The injury wasn't bad. If her parents noticed it or the ones on Len's elbows, they'd assume them to be just some of the hundreds of scrapes and bruises that Len always seemed to have. The life of a toddler was a rough one.

Noe looked at the injury on her own hand. The palm was red and puffy, like she'd burned it on a hot pan. Other than that and a few aches and pains, she'd mostly recovered from the previous night. On her wrist was an almost matching red mark from her nightly binding. She rubbed at it and thought about her parents. They couldn't stop her or Len from being hurt by the Smashed Man. They didn't even seem to want to help with their parasomnia. They thought a baby gate and a locked front door would solve everything. She hugged Len tighter.

"Ow, sissy," said Len, squirming.

Noe let her up. Len tried to gather all three stuffed animals into her arms again and failed. She looked at Noe, who sighed and piled the three animals into her arms for her. "Go play. I need to go somewhere."

Noe got up, threw her dish in the sink, and marched out of the house with Erica's diary in her hand. She crossed the street to Radiah's house. On the way, she glanced at the white house. It looked solid. Real. Like everybody should be able to see it. The black X, the Nonatuke, sparkled on the front of the house.

She knocked on Radiah's door as hard as she could.

"Hello, Miss Christmas," said Radiah's mom after she opened the door.

"Radiah in the attic?"

"She is. Go on up. See if you can't get her to go outside."

Noe walked up the stairs, down the hallway past all the empty rooms, and into Radiah's old room. She knocked on the attic door. It felt silly doing that.

"Yes?" came a soft voice.

"It's Noe." Talking through an attic door felt even sillier.

"What are you doing here?"

"I've got something to show you. Please stop making me talk to an attic door."

"Come on up, I guess," said Radiah.

When they were both in the attic, Radiah sitting on her bed and Noe standing awkwardly in the middle of the room, Radiah asked, "What's that book?"

"Hold on. I need to test something first. Can you look out the window for me?"

Radiah narrowed her eyes. "Why?"

"Just do it, and then I'll explain."

Radiah walked slowly toward the window but kept her eyes on Noe.

"Look out the window," said Noe, walking up behind her.

Radiah complied, but slowly, like she expected Noe to club her over the head. Noe stood beside her and looked into her eyes. "Now look over there at the tip of the dead end." Noe pointed at the white house. Radiah angled her head slightly, and Noe watched her dark brown irises shimmer into unearthly violet. The last time Noe had seen that happen, she had run screaming into her house. It still made her want to. "Okay. Get the other Dread Enders over here. I've got something important to show all of you."

"Tell me first," Radiah said, turning around. Noe watched her irises bleed back to brown.

"Everyone should be here. It's about Erica."

Radiah squinted her eyes at Noe but picked her phone off her bed. The crack in the case had gotten worse, almost splitting it in two. Radiah punched the glass with staccato fingers. A few buzzes later, she said, "Crystal will be here soon. Ruthy doesn't have a phone, so I'll have to go get her. I'll be right back."

"You're really good with Ruthy," said Noe.

Radiah stopped at the top of the stairs but didn't turn around. "I hate the idea of her alone in her house. I remember when I was that young and had to deal with the Smashed Man by myself." Noe thought of Len in the basement with the Smashed Man and nodded, even though Radiah couldn't see her do it.

After Radiah left, Noe looked around the room. Radiah's mom should call her own daughter Miss Christmas. The girl lived up here like a box of decorations. All because a flat monster oozed out of the cracks in her basement. She saw the pencil sketches on the desk and flipped through some of the drawings. There was Ruthy's witch house. Rune Rock. An astronaut floating in space. A herd of horses crossing a stream. Radiah was really good. Noe stopped at a portrait of a girl that Radiah had labeled *Erica.*

Erica had bobbed hair and freckles so big and prominent Radiah must have exaggerated them. And Radiah had drawn her smiling. That made sense to Noe. Based on the diary, she could tell that Erica was different from the other Dread Enders.

Eventually Noe heard commotion downstairs. She tucked the drawing of Erica back underneath the others and quickly settled herself on Radiah's bed. Radiah, Crystal, and Ruthy popped up the stairs and into the room.

"Hi, Noe!" said Ruthy in what was almost a cheery voice. It made Noe sad. If that girl had been born anywhere else but this neighborhood, she would have been such an upbeat, happy girl.

"Hi," she said. She nodded to Crystal.

"Okay," said Radiah. "We're all here. What is that book and what does it have to do with Erica?"

Noe handed the diary to Crystal, who opened it to the first page. Her eyes widened as she read. She sank down onto the edge of the bed, her eyes never leaving the pages. "Oh my gosh" was all she said. Radiah and Ruthy crowded around her.

"It was in the space between the wall and the dryer in my basement," said Noe. "A lot of it is unreadable." Nobody responded. They were engrossed in the messages from their friend. Noe quietly moved away from the group and left the attic and then the house. It was an intimate reunion with a friend they thought they'd never talk to again. They should have privacy. She sat on the front stoop and gazed at the white house.

After a while, the noise of the door opening behind her surprised her into jumping up like she'd been trespassing. Crystal, Radiah, and Ruthy all stood there, their eyes red and faces puffy.

"I'm sorry about your friend," said Noe. "I really am."

"Thanks," said Radiah, rubbing at her eyes. "What was wrong with the ink she used? Why did it all clump up and change color like that?"

"I don't know," said Noe.

Radiah looked around the neighborhood. "So it's over there, I guess?" She pointed uncertainly in the direction of the white house. "An entire house, and we can't see it. Erica was pretty funny. Always joking around."

"I can see it," said Noe.

The Dread Enders all looked at her in surprise.

"That's why I ran away from you last week, like Erica did that one time. I saw your eyes turn purple and thought it was the Smashed Man. I didn't know you couldn't see the house. I didn't know that the runes had any powers."

"Only you and Erica can see this house." Radiah didn't seem to like that idea.

"Can you take us to it?" asked Crystal.

"Wait. What? Don't tell me you're falling for this," said Radiah, waving both of her hands in front of her. "There's no such thing as an invisible house."

"Well, I believe Erica, and it sounds like it has all the answers to the Smashed Man," said Crystal.

"No, even if it does exist, it sounds like it gave Erica all the wrong ideas about the Smashed Man. If she hadn't found what she did there, she'd still be here with us," said Radiah.

"What do you think?" asked Crystal, turning to Noe.

"I think Radiah is right about how much good it did Erica. But it is real. I'm looking directly at it. And now that we all know about it, it's going to drive us crazy knowing it's just sitting there at the end of our neighborhood."

"What if somebody lives there?" Ruthy looked over at the end of the cul-de-sac, fright crossing her face.

"From what we could read of Erica's description, it sounded like nobody lives there," said Crystal.

Noe remembered the movement in the window. The one she had seen when she'd found Ruthy's paper monster at her mailbox. She decided not to bring it up. "There's no harm in at least walking over there, right?" she asked.

"Okay," said Radiah. "But only because there's no such thing as an invisible house and you guys need to see how ridiculous this is."

Noe led them across the bulb of the dead end to the white house, aiming at the shimmery black X like a target. She walked up the steps to the front porch and turned around. The three girls looking up at her had purple eyes.

But what really made her jump was hearing the door behind her open.

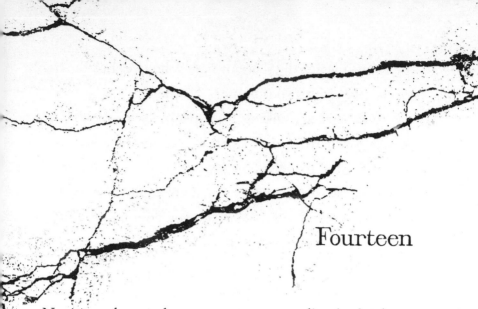

# Fourteen

Noe turned around to see a woman standing in the door-way of the white house. She had short black hair that curled at the ends and a pair of spectacles with large rosy lenses. She wore a bright blue dress and leaned against an aluminum crutch, the top of which wrapped around her forearm. The woman stopped short of exiting the house, standing in the doorway like she wasn't allowed to leave.

"Who are you?" asked Noe.

"Your eyes are normal, girl." She tapped the side of her spectacles as if she wasn't sure if Noe knew what eyes were. She had a Southern accent.

"That's not a name." Noe bristled at how the woman said "girl."

"Who are you talking to?" asked Radiah.

Noe didn't answer. She wasn't sure. Wasn't even sure if

the woman was really there or not. Who lives in an invisible house? "Is this your house?" Noe asked.

"Who are you talking to, Noe?" asked Crystal, her purple eyes darting around the space that Noe saw as a house, but the rest of them saw as forest. Noe shivered, remembering her purple-eyed father standing beside her in the basement asking, "What are you pointing at, Noe?"

"They can't hear you?" asked Noe.

"Does it sound like they can hear me? As long as I stay inside this house, they can't see or hear me. And you shouldn't be able to, either," said the woman with the accent.

"Noe, what is going on!" said Radiah.

"You were spying on me when I went to get the mail the other week," said Noe, guessing that this woman was the one who had moved the curtain.

"A woman can look out her own window."

"Erica was joking, wasn't she? There's no house here. You're messing with us too," said Radiah.

Noe finally gave up on the woman in the invisible house and turned to her purple-eyed friends, startling a bit because she couldn't get used to seeing eyes that color. "There's a house here. And apparently somebody lives in it. That's who I'm talking to. You can't see or hear her because she's inside."

"For goodness' sake," said Radiah, and marched directly at Noe and the house. Except Radiah didn't walk straight. She veered around the house until she ended up at a spot up the ravine. She turned and crossed her arms. Her purple eyes were tiny glowing flecks at this distance. "See? I just walked through it. No house."

"You'll never convince her she's not walking in a straight line." The woman looked around the neighborhood, her eyes squinting behind the tinted lenses. "I can't have you girls drawing attention to this part of the street. Come inside." The woman disappeared into the house, leaving the door open.

After Radiah returned, walking that same curve that didn't seem like a curve to her, Noe said, "I know you can't see it, but there is a house here. And I think it holds the answers to everything. To Erica. To her diary. To this neighborhood. To . . . the Smashed Man. But the only way I'm going to be able to show you is to take you inside." She took Ruthy's hand and then motioned for Crystal and Radiah to form a chain. "Follow me for ten more seconds, and if nothing unusual happens, call me crazy and we can all go home."

The girls all paused, looking at each other uncertainly, before finally linking hands and following Noe. She thought there might be problems going up the steps to the porch, but the girls followed her like they were walking up a hill. She crossed the threshold of the open door and heard a gasp behind her. Her head whipped around, and she saw her purple-eyed friends staring at her hand, the one that held Ruthy's.

*I must have disappeared,* she thought. And then she almost giggled. *Except for my hand.* She tugged Ruthy through, and the other two girls followed.

"Did we just teleport?" asked Crystal, looking around the inside of the house with the wonder of someone who has seen a well-executed magic trick. Her eyes had returned to their bright blue.

"Erica's diary was right," said Radiah, her brown eyes and mouth competing for which was opened wider.

"This place is a dump," said Noe.

Around them were piles of books and laboratory equipment. The peeling walls had star charts and scientific diagrams taped to them. One of the windows had a large, jagged hole in the glass. That must have been from Erica. But mixed in with all that were dirty, rumpled clothes and dishes caked with dried food. There was a rickety folding camp chair. A stained, threadbare couch. It was disgusting. Like the way Mom described Noe's room when it was only messy.

"I hate it here," said the woman with the accent,

appearing from a side room. She was balancing a rattling brass tea set on a platter in one hand, while her other hand was busy with the crutch. She looked precarious, so Noe lifted her arms to help her, but the woman shot her a look through the red lenses that made Noe back up instead. "I can't believe I have to live here. All because of that little girl going after the monster in her basement."

All four girls froze and stared at the woman. "You know about the Smashed Man?" Noe asked.

"Is that what you girls call him?"

"But adults . . ."

"Noelle Wiley, you don't know anything. You've all stumbled across a monster and think you know everything about every universe."

"You're not very nice," said Ruthy.

"Why would I be? A month ago, I was home in Gulf Shores. That's in Alabama. It's the most beautiful place in the country. Right on the bluest part of the Gulf of Mexico. Warm all the time, and sunshine like it's your best friend. White sand so bright and clean. Birds so big they're like angels skimming across the water. And now I'm in this tiny town in cold, gray New England. I mean, you call this summer?" She pointed out the window. "I'm not even breaking a sweat." She shook her head, the curly ends of her hair bobbing a little as she did so. "If only that girl had

125

left the . . . Smashed Man . . . alone."

"I don't like the way this woman is talking about Erica," said Radiah.

"How do you know my name?" asked Noe. "And what's yours?"

"Fern. And I know who you are because it's ridiculously easy to discover that kind of information." Fern placed the tea set on a cardboard box and poured tea into three brass teacups engraved with elephants, the trunks of which formed the cup handles. "Take a cup of tea. Sit down somewhere. I don't like you girls standing around like a bunch of fool flamingos." She didn't acknowledge that there weren't enough teacups for everyone but did take one for herself.

None of the girls took the remaining two teacups, but they all crowded onto the couch after pushing off clothes and moving dishes to the floor. Noe leaned on one of the couch's arms. It looked like it had been clawed by a cat. Fern sat with a little difficulty in the folding camp chair—this time Noe didn't even try to help her—placing the crutch on the floor beside her and holding her cup of tea delicately, like it might disintegrate at any second.

"Let me make this clear: I don't want to explain anything to you," said Fern. "I want you all to go back to your homes and forget about this house. That's what I want most in the world right now. But I also know that's not going to happen. Because little girls like you don't know what's best. So I'm going to explain a few things so that you'll leave me and this house alone. I want you all to shut your mouths. Don't ask questions. Don't comment. And when I'm done, you go home and forget about this house."

Noe didn't like this woman at all, but she would put up with anything to learn more about the Smashed Man.

Fern took a deep breath. "We don't know if we're alone in the universe, but we know that the universe isn't alone. There are billions of universes. But they're not out there." Fern pointed at the ceiling fan, somehow successfully indicating the starry blackness wrapped around the planet. "They're here and there and everywhere." She started pointing randomly around the room with her free hand, somehow successfully indicating the disgusting room around them. "Universes of different sizes overlapping and moving through each other at different speeds, some fast, some slow. You, tall girl, raise your hand." Crystal did so, slowly. "A universe the size of a baseball just passed through your palm. You, little girl, stand up." Ruthy jumped up like she was in trouble. "A universe the size of a marble just moved through your stomach. And in about five seconds, a universe the size of a whale will have finished passing through the whole house after starting about ten minutes ago." She paused while Ruthy sat back down and they all stared around the room, waiting to feel the whale. "And that was three of about seven thousand universes that are moving past us right now in all directions."

"You can see all that?" asked Noe doubtfully, still looking around the room.

"I said no questions, girl." Fern's eyes narrowed, like she was trying to shoot lasers at Noe through her lenses. "Especially silly ones. Nobody can see them." Fern grabbed her teacup by the elephant trunk and took a loud sip.

"The universe is infinite." That came from Crystal, and the other girls looked at her in surprise.

"You girls just won't listen," said Fern. "An infinite universe is conventional science. That doesn't apply here. What would your science teacher say to a two-dimensional monster coming through a crack in your basement wall, huh?" Crystal shook her head slowly. Noe looked over at her in sympathy. As strange as it was for Noe to hear an adult talk about the Smashed Man, it must have been a thousand times stranger for the other Dread Enders, who had waited their whole lives for an adult to acknowledge the monster in their basements. "Conventional science deals with observable phenomena. When you can't observe things because your eyes go all indigo . . ." Fern shrugged and took another sip of tea.

"What do all your universes have to do with the monster in our basements?" asked Noe.

"Everything," said Fern, her lenses firing up again. "Sometimes a universe or a part of a universe gets caught inside another. It doesn't flow through. It stops, like one fist inside another." She held up a fist, but her other was clenching a teacup, so she dropped the fist to her lap. "We call them stuck places. And there's a stuck place under Totter Court."

Had Noe not seen a flat monster sliding out of a crack in her basement and people's eyes turning purple and an invisible house, she would have called this woman crazy and run back home. She snuck a glance at the other Dread Enders. They were listening with full attention. They wanted answers badly.

"How long has it been under there?" asked Noe.

"I don't know. At least a couple of decades, I think. Not a very relevant question."

Noe bristled like when Fern called her "girl."

"Is that where the Smashed Man is coming from? This stuck place?"

Fern emptied the cup of tea and put it back on the tray. She hesitated a moment, throwing a quick glance at the girls, and then picked up another. "That's a better question. But no."

"Where does he come from, then?"

Fern scratched at her ear. Adjusted her glasses. Ran her finger along the rim of the teacup. She was obviously trying to figure out what she was going to tell them. Finally she said, "This is where what we know gets . . . wiggly. We think that when one place gets stuck in another, there's still some space between them, a zone of limbo between the two. And that's where the Smashed Man lives. At least when he's not trying to get through to our world. That's why 'Smashed Man' is such an interesting phrase to me. He really is smashed between two places."

Noe was about to fire off another question when she realized that she had been asking all the questions so far. She looked over at the other girls on the couch. They were all still staring at Fern. And they looked more fragile than usual. Radiah's eyes were watery. Ruthy was sunk into the cushions. Crystal looked sunk within herself. They wanted the answers so badly but were also afraid of those answers. The answers could make things worse. They couldn't take worse. Noe asked another question.

"Why is he trying to get through to our world?"

"I don't know."

"What will happen if he does?"

"I don't know."

"What happened to Erica?"

"I don't know."

It felt like the first time she had visited Rune Rock with the Dread Enders. Nobody knew anything. "What do you know?"

Fern laughed. A short, loud bark. "More than you, but not much more. We're bumbling along, really."

"Who is *we*?" asked Radiah.

"There is a small group of us that are not susceptible to the violet blindness as adults. We don't know why. We call ourselves the Neighbors. We observe stuck places."

When Noe pulled out her phone, she said, "You won't find anything about us online, girl. Not with a name as common as ours. That's why we chose it. Just like you won't find anything about two-dimensional basement monsters."

"So you're not here to . . . fix everything?" That was Ruthy, and the way she said it almost broke Noe's heart.

"I'm not a handyman, little girl."

"You barely know anything. Why are you even here?" asked Noe, angry at the way she talked to Ruthy.

"This is what comes from asking too many questions and not listening. As I just said, I'm here to observe. This house is an observation post. We have one everywhere we discover a stuck place. But nobody has been at this post for a long time. No reason to be. Until that girl in the red house did whatever she did. Do you know what she did?"

"No," said Radiah. *Good idea,* thought Noe. No reason to tell this woman anything.

"So what's different about you, Noelle Wiley? How come you can see past the Nonatuke?" Fern looked at Noe over the rim of her teacup. Noe decided to pick the last cup up for herself. Not because she wanted tea, but because she felt like she needed a buffer between her and this woman. The tea wasn't dark brown like she expected. It was almost white. She took a sip. It was thick and tasted sweet and spicy. It was wonderful.

"It's chai. And not that sugary milk most people call chai. This is straight from India. Too good for you."

Noe took another sip.

"Do you have autism? Asthma? An oversized birthmark?" Fern asked.

"There's nothing wrong with me."

"I didn't ask if anything was wrong with you. You think this is something wrong with me?" She gently kicked the aluminum shaft lying beside her. "I asked if anything was *different* about you. Peanut allergy? Heart murmur?"

"No." She tried to be as definite with the answer as Radiah had been.

"There is something, even if you don't know what it is. It's what makes you able to see this house. To see past the Nonatuke painted on it."

"Nonatuke." Noe took her time with the word, like it was the first time she had ever come across those syllables. It wasn't hard to fake. The word was hard to say. "That X on the front of the house? It's painted with the same sparkly stuff that's on the Dead End sign and on Rune Rock. What is all that?"

"Rune Rock?" Fern thought for a bit. "Oh, one of the sigils out in the forest. You girls have a gift with naming. You know what a sigil is? It's kind of a magic symbol. Not that we believe in magic, but it seems to fit here, because those sigils have some kind of power when painted with darkwash. A power we don't always understand."

"Darkwash?"

"It's a by-product of a place getting stuck within another. One of the Neighbors figured out how to collect it from between the stuck places. The same space where the Smashed Man lives." Fern reached down and plucked a thin, tall glass vial about the length of her hand from a pile of books and old soda cans and other vials. The glass tube was full of dark liquid with tiny bright specks of light. They seemed to be moving. The star stuff Erica had mentioned in her diary.

"What does the R sigil do?" asked Noe. "The one on Rune Rock?"

"It's not an R. It's an Amberonk. A very old sigil. The Egyptians used it. They called it the Eye of Horus. Or t'

Eye of Ra. I forget which is which. It's the one that looks like a right eye." Fern placed her left hand over the left lens of her glasses. "I suspect they knew about stuck places."

"But what does it do?" asked Noe, who didn't want a history lesson.

"It's for protection," said Fern. "We use it to mark the border of the stuck place." She shrugged her shoulders and took a sip of tea.

"What do you and the Neighbors plan to do here?" asked Crystal, stumbling over "Neighbors," like she felt wrong using the word that way.

"Nothing,"

"Nothing?" said Ruthy.

"That's right. Nothing. Same as you girls should do. Leave me alone. Leave the Smashed Man alone. Let me finish my observations so I can go back to Gulf Shores and have a decent sweat."

Noe jumped up, angry, "Well, if you're not going to be any help, then we should just go. . . ." As Noe said it, she dropped her half-full elephant teacup too hard on the tray, stumbling into it at the same time. The whole set clashed wetly to the ground, with Noe following it.

"Careful, girl!" Fern bent down and started picking up the cups and mopping up chai with a navy-blue T-shirt that was lying on the floor. "That tea set survived all the way from India to Gulf Shores to here, but it's no match for a bunch of clumsy New England girls."

Noe picked herself off the floor. "Let's go," she said to the Dread Enders.

"But . . . ," started Radiah, but she didn't finish because Noe was already opening the door to leave. Radiah took one more look at the woman, who was holding the elephant teapot up to her red glasses, scouring it for any cracks or dents, and then followed Noe, the other girls right behind her.

"Don't come back," Fern yelled after them.

Noe shut the door. Outside, she watched the other girls pause like they'd been dropped there from the sky, dazed and uncertain. They stared at where the house was. Their irises were purple.

Noe whispered, "Let's go to Rune Rock."

"Why?" asked Radiah, slowly coming out of her daze.

"Because I have a plan to get rid of the Smashed Man." Noe lifted up the front of her shirt about an inch, revealing the tip of a vial of darkwash sticking out from her waistband.

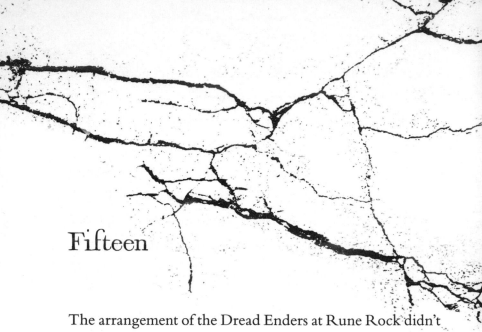

# Fifteen

The arrangement of the Dread Enders at Rune Rock didn't feel like a courtroom to Noe this time. That was because she was the one atop the rock with the sparkly R on it . . . the darkwash Amberonk. Everyone else sat below her on the logs and leaves and moss. The scene might have been pleasant, like a picnic, were the other girls not looking up at her in horror.

Noe had just laid out her plan to rid Totter Court of the Smashed Man.

"No. No. No. No, Noe," said Radiah, breaking a thin pine branch in her hands. "We do what we always do. We do what that woman said. We get through it. We stay out of our basements at night. We grow up. We move away. We forget about the Smashed Man forever."

"It's worked for us so far," said Crystal.

"I can't do that," said Noe. "I can't do that at all."

"You sound like Erica," said Ruthy.

"Yeah, she went at the Smashed Man instead of avoiding him," said Radiah. "And look where she is now."

Noe stared down at the shimmering sigil of protection on the smooth hunk of moss-covered granite. They had barely talked about Fern. Nobody knew whether to believe her or not, and even if they did, it didn't change anything. They hadn't learned anything that would help them. There was still a monster in their basements. One that had gotten Erica. Next would be Noe. Or Len.

Noe's shoulders slumped, and she said, "I'm not trying to be brave. Or make drama. Or pretend to know better than anybody else here." She swallowed. Her throat felt thick, like she was about to vomit. "If I don't destroy the Smashed Man, he'll get me. And my little sister. And probably the rest of you after that."

"What do you mean?" asked Crystal.

Noe swallowed again. She stared down at the vial of darkwash in her hand. The bright specks swam through the darkness like glowing fish in an ocean. She had never had to tell anybody about her parasomnia before. The only people who knew were her family and her doctors. Abby's family knew too, but she didn't have to tell them. They'd found out the hard way.

Abby was the last person she wanted to think about right at this moment. Parasomnia had ended their friendship, even though it wasn't Noe's fault. Even though she couldn't help herself. Could these new girls trust her? They'd spent their entire lives being so careful to avoid the Smashed Man, and here she moves in and could free him on any night without even realizing it. She took a deep breath and looked from one girl to the other. "I have a medical condition."

The other girls looked at her expectantly, with concern and not a little bit of fear.

"Sometimes my sleep cycle is interrupted. During the non-REM stage, I . . ." She trailed off. Why was she using doctor words? She dropped her head and looked at the forest floor. "I sleepwalk."

When she didn't hear a response, she looked up. The girls were staring at her, confusion on their faces. Crystal was the one who broke the awkwardness.

"I grind my teeth in my sleep. Sometimes I wake up with awful headaches from it. My dentist wants me to wear a mouth guard every night, but it makes me feel like I'm suffocating."

Noe was confused by Crystal's admission at first, but then realized that she was trying to make her feel better about her own medical condition. "Thanks, but that's not what I mean. I mean that any night I can end up in the basement. Without realizing it. I can get up, walk down there, and stand until the Smashed Man comes out. All while asleep. It's already gotten close to happening."

Ruthy gasped. Radiah dropped the two pieces of pine branch that she had been rubbing together as if she was trying to start a fire. Crystal stared at Noe like she was seeing her for the first time.

"It gets worse. Since we moved to this new house, Len has started sleepwalking. I found her the other night inches away from the Smashed Man. He was almost out. I grabbed Len and somehow touched him." She held up her hands to show the red welt on her palm. "We were both thrown across the basement. It felt like . . . I don't know what it felt like. But it hurt." She took a shaky breath. "I'm sorry. Sorry that you all have had to live with the Smashed Man. Sorry about what happened to Erica. Sorry that Len and I moved here and now everybody's in danger. I'm sorry." Tears welled in her eyes and dropped to the stone. It felt like Abby all over again.

"It's not your fault."

Noe's head shot up, not because of what was said, but because of who had said it. Radiah continued. "I told you before, you're one of us, whether you like it or not. You're a Dread Ender." She stood up from where she had been sitting on the forest floor. "And now we know what's different about you."

"What do you mean?" asked Noe.

"What Fern said. What's different about you, that you can see past the Nonatuke." Noe didn't know what to say to that, so she just stayed silent and let Radiah keep talking. "How do you know that this plan will work?"

Noe slid down the rock and stood with the other Dread Enders. She knew what to say to that. "Erica was confident she finally had a plan that could beat him. I don't know why she was so confident, but I believe her."

"But she was wrong," said Radiah.

"And how can you even know her plan? Most of her diary is just splotches of . . . darkwash," said Crystal, looking at the vial in Noe's hand.

"Enough of it is there. And I also think that she didn't have all the information she needed for her plan."

"You know something she didn't?" asked Radiah.

"I do. Or at least I think I do. Remember the first time you took me here to Rune Rock? I told you about going down into the basement on the night I moved in."

"You didn't see the Smashed Man," said Ruthy.

"I thought you were being a jerk," said Radiah.

Noe laughed. "I was probably being a little bit of a jerk, but that's exactly what happened. I went down there, and

140

the Smashed Man didn't come out. It was the only time that happened. Erica said in her diary that she was going to wait until the Smashed Man came almost all the way out, because she thought that would weaken him. I think she was right. I think that it must take a lot of energy for the Smashed Man to come into our basements, especially now that we know he's slipping into our world from outside it. I also think Erica might have weakened him further doing whatever she did. That's maybe why she's still alive. That's maybe why he wasn't in the basement the first night I went down there. He was too weak to come through.

"By the time I went down there again a week later—which would have been more than a month after Erica's incident—he had recovered. If we work together, we can weaken the Smashed Man even more. And once he's at his weakest, I can put Erica's plan into action. I can paint the Elberex on his head with this darkwash." She held out the vial in the palm of her hand. It shimmered strangely. Noe had to admit to herself that it seemed too small in that giant forest to be the answer they were looking for.

"And we'll never have to worry about the Smashed Man again," said Ruthy, as if she couldn't believe it either.

"Should we get help from Fern?" asked Crystal. "I don't like her, but she's the only adult here who knows about the Smashed Man."

"That woman doesn't know anything," said Radiah. "Her and her stupid Neighbors or whatever have known about the Smashed Man for a long time, and they haven't done a single thing about him. She might as well be purple eyed like the rest of the adults. Plus, she's just mean."

"What if it doesn't work?" asked Crystal.

Noe thought for a moment before replying. "Then you won't have to worry about my sleepwalking letting him out anymore."

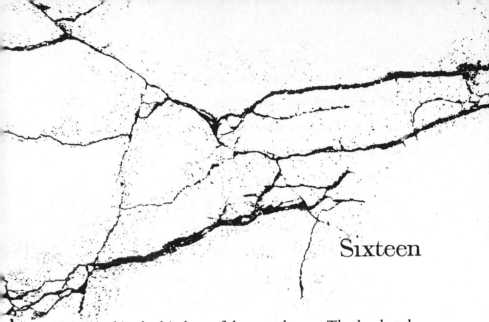

# Sixteen

Noe stood in the kitchen of the new house. That's what she still called it. The new house. Not *the* house or *her* house. Not even the *red* house. It was the new house. Everything was new. She had only been living here for about a month, but in that month everything had changed. The people in her life were completely different. What she saw outside her window was completely different. What she felt inside was completely different. The nature of the universe itself was completely different. And all she'd done was move from one house to another.

Behind Noe was a square of darkness, in front of her a rectangle of darkness. The darkness behind her was the window. Pitch-black like the glass was painted over. Midnight, according to the glowing numerals on her phone. That was the part that should have been scary, that square of darkness. The woods. The night. The outside. All the things Len—and any other child with any sense—would be scared of. But instead, it was the black rectangle in front of her that was scary to Noe. The basement door. The basement door that she was about to open.

But for the first time, she felt a good kind of scared again. The exhilarated kind of scared. The type of scared that you know you'll be better for when it's over. You just have to get through that type of scared, and your life gets better. Most important, she was about to do something. To take control of something in her life. She couldn't control where she went when she sleepwalked. She couldn't fight her night terrors. It all made her feel so helpless. But soon she was going to walk right downstairs and fight the monster in the basement. Or at least try to.

Noe pulled her phone from her pocket and hit the chat icon. The app opened, and she selected the group chat option. **Ready**, she tapped, the word popping up in the message screen beside her avatar, a picture of the new house. Her avatar was usually a Great Dane, the exact dog she was hoping to get at this new house with its big backyard before her priorities changed. She'd replaced her avatar for tonight.

A trio of dots danced in the message screen beside Radiah's blue house, telling her Radiah was responding.

**We're both here** popped up. The "both" was Radiah and Ruthy. They were going to do this together, even though Ruthy had argued with them about it. It would have been nice to have one more basement in play, but no way were they going to put Ruthy in danger by herself. It was easy to arrange. Ruthy slept over at Radiah's house regularly.

No dots danced after that. When the time in the corner of her phone changed to 12:03, Noe typed, **Crystal?** Normally, three minutes late wouldn't be worrisome, but tonight would require precision.

It wasn't until 12:05 that dots started dancing by the avatar of the yellow house, Crystal's house. **Here. Sorry.** It was followed by a toilet emoji.

Noe typed, **Me first. Then R&R. Then C. Handoff word is OUT.**

**OK,** said the blue house.

**OK,** said the yellow house.

**OK,** she typed back.

Texting wasn't ideal. Not for this kind of situation. Noe had wanted to do a group video chat, but the signal in their basements wasn't great, and it might be too loud. They couldn't risk waking up their parents.

Noe touched the back pocket of her jeans and felt the tall lump from the vial of darkwash. She had already made sure that Len's door was shut and that the baby gate was locked. She had even tied the sash of her robe around the baby gate latch to make double sure it was secure. She couldn't have Len interrupt her any more than Mom and Dad. She typed the word **OUT** into the message field of the app but didn't hit send. She opened the black door, took a deep breath, and descended into the basement.

The space below her new house never seemed to be any different. Only the rise and fall of the piles of laundry in the baskets in front of the washer and dryer signaled the changing of time down here. Noe suddenly felt as if she were on an alien world. The hard-packed dirt under her sneakers was virgin soil. The rock walls surrounding her were unexplored ruins. She walked gingerly around the furnace and water heater, alien artifacts on this distant planet.

She stopped about ten feet from the giant crack—a crack not just in the wall, but in the substance of the universe, in the happiness of her life. She planted herself in front of the crack, but as far back as she could be, her back against the water heater like it was a jet pack ready to rocket her through two floors and into the night sky if she needed to escape.

The Smashed Man started oozing.

Even though she had seen it happen three times now, she couldn't get used it. The impossibility of something fitting through that crack. The slowness of it. The silence of it. The exacting loop of it all. The horrid expression on his face when it tipped up. *Here we are again,* he seemed to say to her. *But this time, I'll get all the way out. Get my flat arms around you. I'll escape the wall, but you will not escape me.* The Smashed Man flowed toward her like it was the first time he had ever done so, that terrible smile on his face like he knew he would eventually get her, even if it took years.

And Noe stood there. Like she'd given up. Like she was rooting for him. Like freeing the Smashed Man was why she had moved to this house in the first place.

But it was hard. She had to fight the impulse to run across the basement. To run up the stairs. To run to Len's bedroom and dive into her bed and cradle her little sister like she was one of Len's stuffed animals. She wanted to run out the front door into the neighborhood, screaming her lungs into her throat. She wanted out of this house. Out of this neighborhood. Out of this town.

But she stood here, her back to the water heater, and faced the Smashed Man.

His face turned up, and she stood there.

His arms freed themselves from the wall, and she stood there.

He reached out to grab her, every minute moving a fraction of an inch closer, and she stood there.

When the only parts of the Smashed Man still in the

wall were the parts of his legs below the knees, when he was almost completely inside her basement, her house, her world, Noe ran. She didn't look back at the Smashed Man. Just ran. Ran until dirt turned to wooden steps turned to vinyl floor. She shut the door and hit send on her phone.

**OUT**


Radiah and Ruthy sat at the kitchen table in Radiah's house. Radiah stared at the dark phone on the table. Ruthy was cutting out a construction-paper Smashed Man. She had a small stack of gray sheets in front of her, held down by a pair of worn purple and red crayons. Behind Radiah, a door was half ajar, showing the hint of carpeted steps angling downward.

Radiah's basement door was between the kitchen and the family room. Radiah hated to even cross the border it marked between the two rooms, much less go down the stairs. She looked at Ruthy, who was lost in the slide of her scissors across the gray paper, and wondered again if she should have made the six-year-old stay at home instead of involving her in this crazy, desperate plan. But that could have led to bigger trouble. Radiah could imagine Ruthy sneaking down to her basement by herself to help the rest of the Dread Enders. Radiah couldn't have risked that, so she was keeping Ruthy close tonight, even if she had to sit here and watch her make those stupid paper Smashed Men all night.

They were both silent, although unlike Noe in her house, they didn't have a reason to be. Radiah's parents slept to the noise of a giant box fan, even in winter. It sounded like a helicopter. Radiah could have invited the circus over and her parents wouldn't have known.

The phone on the table buzzed loudly and the screen lit up in glaring digital brightness in the dim kitchen. Radiah jumped and Ruthy dropped the scissors onto the table. A single word stood out in all caps beside the avatar of a red house: **OUT**. Radiah felt like she was going to puke.

Ruthy seemed less affected. She grabbed Radiah's phone and typed **OK**, then jumped to her feet, her half-finished Smashed Man fluttering slowly to the ground. Radiah barely had time to pick up the phone before Ruthy grabbed her hand and led her toward the basement.

At the door, Radiah took the lead. She wasn't going to let a six-year-old outbrave her, nor was she going to let the newcomer to the neighborhood do it either. Not to mention that for the plan to work, it was important that they get downstairs as fast as possible, now that they had the message from Noe.

Radiah and Ruthy thumped down the carpeted steps to the basement. The room looked like it hadn't been decorated since the previous millennium. The floor was a thick green carpet that could swallow a person's foot to the ankle. The walls were covered in dark fake-wood paneling that was stained two feet from the floor by some distant flood that had happened before Radiah was born. At one time, judging from the covered pool table and the couch in its center and the large CD player, the basement had been a fun room to hang out in. These days, it was storage. The couch and the pool table and the floor were piled high with cardboard boxes and stacks of magazines and various pieces of past lives lived. The entire basement was one big history lesson.

But the girls weren't paying attention to the room. Their eyes were drawn as if attached by threads to a single spot on the wall behind the couch. A two-foot-wide section of paneling was missing, exposing bare concrete behind it. In the concrete was a vertical fracture that stretched from ceiling to floor. The long crack had been there for Radiah's entire life. Her mother and father had never brought it up. Probably didn't notice it.

Within ten seconds of them looking at the crack, the Smashed Man started oozing. He came out sideways, since the crack was almost a straight line up and down. They watched the thin blade of his body split the air, emerging so slowly it was as if he wasn't moving at all.

Time felt different in front of the Smashed Man. Radiah thought that terror clouded her sense of time, but if what Fern had said was true, it might be actual physics. Noe and Crystal could be waiting by their basement doors for seconds while she and Ruthy experienced the Smashed Man's slow squeeze through the wall over hours or days or years. None of the Dread Enders had ever timed it before. None of the Dread Enders had ever had a reason to.

His head lifted sideways, his face leering at the two girls as if he was happy to see them, happy to terrify them. By the time he was halfway out, he had twisted his body so that his upper half was parallel to the floor. The whole thing was a scene Radiah knew too well. It played for her every night in nightmares in the attic. Like an old, traumatic memory relived over and over again, inescapable.

Radiah gripped her phone with the cracked case in one hand and Ruthy's tiny, soft hand in the other. The younger girl looked mesmerized, like a mouse in front of a cobra. If Radiah didn't make her leave, she might stay until the monster freed itself from the wall.

And it was getting close to doing exactly that.

"We should go now, right?" said Ruthy, shaking her friend's hand but not able to tear her eyes away from the horrible spectacle of the flat monster coming out of the wall. The Dread Enders had decided that each girl was to wait until the Smashed Man was freed to midcalf before fleeing their basements.

"Not yet," said Radiah, not taking her eyes off the fiend. She wanted to one-up Noe.

"But he's almost to his ankles!" said Ruthy.

"Hold on," said Radiah, priming her body for action.

When he was only three inches from leaving the wall, Radiah shouted, "Now!" and pulled Ruthy hard toward the stairs. She was halfway up when she turned to see that Ruthy, even though she had followed along, was still staring back at the Smashed Man over her shoulder, which slowed her down, even as Radiah tugged at her hand.

"Look away from him, Ruthy! Go faster!" That snapped the younger girl out of it. Ruthy looked up at Radiah, and the two continued up the stairs to the kitchen. Radiah slammed the door, and they both dropped to the floor, their backs against the door as if they were afraid the Smashed Man would try to break it down. They were sweating and breathing hard. They had definitely made enough noise to have woken Radiah's parents if it weren't for the box fan.

Radiah hit three letters into her phone with a trembling finger and hit the send button.

**OUT**

★ ★ ★

152

Crystal stood in the hallway, where the door to the basement loomed. It looked like all the other doors in the hallway, warm brown wood with a shiny brass knob. She chewed on the nail of her index finger. She didn't want to go down there. Even if there had been no such thing as the Smashed Man, she still wouldn't have wanted to go down there. That was where the schoolroom was. Her isolated little schoolroom. It might not be so bad, had her mom not set it up to look like a real schoolroom. Like it was a parody of one. On the walls there was a map of Europe and a poster of the periodic table and a photo of the cathedral-like interior of the Trinity College library in Ireland. In the corner was a whiteboard on wheels, and against a wall was a shelf with all her schoolbooks on it. Worse, in the center of the room was a lonely little wooden desk for her.

Being homeschooled embarrassed her. And not just because Radiah and Ruthy and Erica made fun of her sometimes. That was fine. They would also say that they were jealous that she didn't have to walk to school in winter, that it only took her three hours to get through her lessons, that she was done with school a good month before any of them and didn't have to go back until a month later.

But homeschooling was lonely, especially with Brett gone. And she was sick of that basement . . . and its monster.

Even though the Smashed Man only came out at night, she always looked for him during class, waiting for him to emerge from the crack in the old plaster that wended around the map of Europe. She took so many bathroom breaks upstairs that her mother once took her to the doctor to see if she had diabetes.

Crystal's phone shook and lit up in her hand. For a few seconds she hoped that the message on the screen was Noe or Radiah calling off the plan. Her heart sank when she saw that it was the handoff word from Radiah. It was Crystal's turn. She typed **OK** into the messaging screen.

Crystal opened the door and gazed down into the darkness. The light switch was at the base of the steps. She had to walk in the dark before she could get to the light. She took the steps down carefully, but when she hit the bottom, her hand scrabbled across the wall frantically until it found the switch. She hit it hard. Her pathetic little class-room appeared before her.

She hadn't been down in the basement since the end of the school year. She walked to the desk in the center of the room. Had it been a desk in a real school, its underside would have been carved with an alphabet soup of initials and names—everyone who had used it before her. But under this desk, there was only one name: Brett Fenwick.

Brett was high school age by the time Crystal started

homeschool. And he really hated homeschool. Crystal didn't know if he had always hated it or only as he got older or if it was just the Smashed Man he hated. She remembered him fighting with her mom a lot, though. Crystal had asked him once if he had seen the Smashed Man, but he acted like he didn't know what she was talking about. Radiah thought it was because he had gotten too old and had forgotten about it. He must have forgotten about it. He wouldn't have gone off to college across the country and left her here to face the Smashed Man alone.

The telltale shimmering of the Smashed Man started under the map of Europe, in line with the boot of Italy. The shimmering turned into a shape as the Smashed Man slid smoothly out, like she envisioned him doing every day during class, behind where her mother stood when she was teaching. It was horrible. She chewed on her index finger. Wished she was with Ruthy and Radiah. Wished she was with Noe. Wished she was with Erica. Wished she was with Brett. The monster's head was out now, and just as it started turning up to face her, she realized she couldn't look at its face. The bruises and the lacerations, the broken teeth, the purple eyes.

Crystal turned and ran up the stairs, closing the door to the basement behind her. She leaned against it and started to cry. Because she was scared. Because she had failed at her task. Even though six-year-old Ruthy could do it. Even though the new girl who had only lived in the neighborhood a month could do it. As she cried, she watched the time on her phone. She had only been down in the basement for a few minutes, not near long enough to draw the Smashed Man out as far as the other girls, so she sat in the hall and waited. Waited until it had been about the same length of time as between the time signatures on Noe's and Radiah's texts before she typed three letters into her phone and hit send.

**OUT**

Noe stared at her phone, waiting for the next message. She yawned hard enough to pop her jaw. Her phone and the microwave across the kitchen agreed that it was almost five in the morning, although the dark window above the sink stayed neutral on the matter. The Dread Enders had been taking turns teasing out the Smashed Man for five hours. That meant Noe, Radiah and Ruthy, and Crystal had each been down in their basements four different times that night, four different cycles of the Smashed Man being drawn from four different basement walls. The first cycle had lasted about an hour, so twenty minutes per basement, although the timing was never exact. Whether that was due to the Dread Enders or the Smashed Man, Noe wasn't sure. As the night wore on, the Smashed Man definitely took longer to unspool. Hopefully that meant he was weakening. Like she believed he would. Like Erica had believed.

Noe wondered if everybody was as beat as she was. This was one of the many parts of the plan that she was worried about, that someone would fall asleep. She looked at the dark window again. It would be sunrise soon. Hers would be the last basement foray of the night, for any of the Dread Enders.

A little sooner than she thought it should, the phone buzzed. Crystal was handing the baton to Noe one last time. Noe typed back the final code word: **ELBEREX**. If things went well, she would send another message in about twenty minutes: **PARTY**.

She put the phone in her pocket and pulled out the vial of darkwash and a thin paintbrush from a watercolor set. She headed down into the basement, put her back against the water heater, and waited for the Smashed Man to unfurl, hopefully for the last time ever on Totter Court.

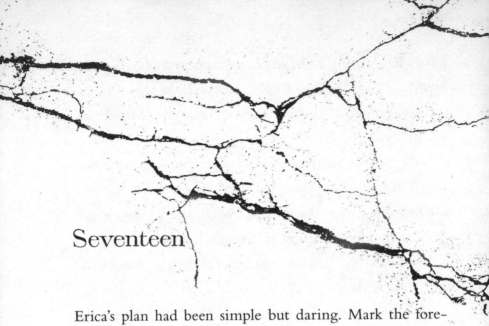

# Seventeen

Erica's plan had been simple but daring. Mark the forehead of the Smashed Man with the darkwash Elberex. Noe
hadn't understood when she first read the diary why Erica
was so confident about the plan. And, Noe had to admit,
she still didn't. Noe didn't feel that confidence, despite what
she had told the other Dread Enders. What she felt was
desperation. There was no other plan. No other choice. It
was this or wait for the Smashed Man to get her while she
was sleepwalking. Or Len.

But the time for thinking about the plan was over.

The crack in the basement wall glistened. The familiar
shape of the Smashed Man's head, especially after the past
five hours, started creeping out, slower than usual. Much
slower than usual. That was a good sign.

Noe opened the glass vial and dropped its small stopper

to the hard dirt below. She took the thin paintbrush and eased it into the sparkly darkwash. It felt like she was sheathing a sword, getting it ready for battle. She felt a little silly with her tiny paintbrush weapon, but no way was she going to touch the Smashed Man with her hand. Not after last time. Her hand still throbbed.

The worst part about watching the Smashed Man creep out of the wall was when he first showed his face. The awful bruised look. The open wounds and torn gray skin. The glistening bone showing through. Those purple shimmering eyes that didn't blink and seemed larger than they should be. That awful jagged smile.

But its silence was the worst.

After a long time, the Smashed Man's face bent up and looked at her. Its expression was the same. As if it didn't know or didn't care that the Dread Enders had been luring him out all night.

Noe had a decision to make. Do it now or wait as long as possible, to weaken him further. She couldn't let him get too far out this time, because of his arms. She couldn't get close enough to his head if his hands were free. But she could wait a little longer. Maybe until he was free to the elbows.

She took a few steps toward him, remembering how close Dad had gotten without seeing him that first time.

The Smashed Man was out past his shoulders now, the gray rags embedded in his grayish skin like old grave clothes. *Sixty more seconds,* she told herself. *Then I do it. For Len. For me. For the rest of the Dread Enders. For Erica.* A type of scared she hadn't felt before filled her stomach and head and made her arms and legs tingle. She counted down in her head.

Fifty seconds.

Forty seconds.

Thirty seconds. She almost wanted to count out loud just to destroy the eerie silence. To see if she could wipe that deranged look off the Smashed Man's flat face.

Twenty seconds. She could hear the plastic handle of the paintbrush tinkling in the jar and realized she was shaking.

Ten seconds. She took a deep breath, unsheathed the paintbrush, the darkwash at its tip dripping a little onto the dirt floor, and then moved toward the Smashed Man's head.

He moved.

The Smashed Man's face didn't change. It stayed maddeningly the same. But the Smashed Man's flat head twisted on his flat neck like he was about to bite her hand. She reacted without thinking, moving her hand out of the way fast and dropping the paintbrush onto the packed dirt.

160

Directly under the Smashed Man.

She almost dived for it in panic but quickly realized that she couldn't go under him. Even without his hands free, he could bend down and get her. His wrists were almost free. She had to act fast, or she'd have to give up and run upstairs and the whole night would be for nothing.

Noe turned the vial of darkwash upside down over her palm. But the liquid was taking too much time to flow out of the thin bottle. She turned around and hit the vial against the metal hide of the water heater. A loud clang filled the basement, but the vial didn't break. She did it again, and this time the clang was accompanied by a sharp tinkling as the vial smashed. The darkwash was all over the side of the water heater, thick and starry. She swiped her right hand through it. The liquid felt prickly. Not painful, but like any moment it could be.

She turned around and extended her index finger, which was coated in a tiny black universe, toward the Smashed Man's forehead. And then she remembered what had happened to her the last time she had touched the Smashed Man.

She drew her hand back fast and looked frantically around the basement for anything she could use to draw the Elberex with. Nothing but laundry and moving boxes. And she didn't have time to dig through moving boxes.

His fingertips were almost out of the wall.

Noe extended the finger and steeled herself, drawing the Elberex on his forehead in one fast sweeping motion. She drew her hand back, almost surprised it was still at the end of her arm, and definitely surprised that she wasn't flung across the room.

For the first time, the Smashed Man's face changed. It looked surprised. It looked pained. The Elberex was working. Noe stood there, her eyes wide, not knowing what was going to happen next. Hoping he'd shrivel back into the wall or disappear. She smelled the faint sweet smell of something burning.

And then pain shot through her left arm like it had been tied to her headboard all night. She yelled, and it went numb.

And the monster's face settled back into his ghastly grimace.

Noe looked down and saw that he had gotten a hand out of the wall and had clamped down on her left wrist. He was using it to pull himself out of the wall faster. He didn't feel weak.

She tried to pull away, but he only came out of the wall more quickly. His hips, his thighs, his calves. He was almost all the way out.

Noe screamed as loud as she could and reached with

her other hand, the one covered in darkwash, and grabbed his face. She felt it bend under her hand like a paper plate, and then she felt him twist out of her grasp. As he did so, his hand loosened on her wrist. She pulled it away and fell onto the packed dirt, dinging her head against the water heater painfully.

She crawled backward, staring at the Smashed Man, who was trying to claw the darkwash off his face. His eyes and teeth showed through it ferociously. The scent of burning intensified.

And then the Smashed Man righted himself.

He stood up in the basement. His legs wobbling, his arms wobbling, every part of him wobbling.

He was completely free of the crack in the wall. And the lurid smile on his darkwash-stained face grew larger.

Noe screamed again and ran upstairs. She grabbed Len out of her bed with her good arm and ran her into her parents' room, still screaming. She pushed Len at her parents' bed and then slammed the door shut.

Her parents awoke in alarm, asking muffled, confused questions.

Noe waited for the Smashed Man to come. To slide through the crack beneath the door. To rise from a gap between the floorboards.

# Eighteen

The Smashed Man didn't appear.

Noe realized in the gradually growing morning light that maybe it was *because* of the gradually growing morning light. They had timed the plan to end right before dawn to maximize how many times they could pull him out of the crack to weaken him, and they had timed it exactly right.

Monsters had rules. And the Smashed Man couldn't do anything during the day.

Still, Noe wouldn't go back to her bedroom. Wouldn't allow her parents to send Len back to hers either. So they all finished the early morning sleeping together in her parents' bed. Except Noe. She didn't sleep. She found herself still waiting for the Smashed Man. Maybe the rules had changed now that he was out of the crack. Now that he was in this world. Her eyes darted to the slit under the door and the space behind the tall dresser. She waited for him to rise at the foot of the bed. She was exhausted, but still she waited, holding Mom until Mom grew uncomfortable and shook her off. The same with Dad. And then Len. And then she had nobody to hold but herself, so she lay there and waited by herself, not feeling more secure just because her entire family was inches away from her.

But the Smashed Man never came.

She reached for her phone to message the other Dread Enders but realized she had dropped it in the basement. She snuck Mom's off her nightstand to let the other Dread Enders know that not only had the plan failed, they were all in danger. They decided to meet at Rune Rock later. She had just deleted the texts so that Mom wouldn't find them when exhaustion landed heavily on her and she finally fell sleep.

When she awoke, she was sweaty, alone, and the gradually growing morning light had been turned up into blazing summer noon. She got up, changed into drier clothes, and headed for Rune Rock.

She was the first to arrive. The air was hot and still. The bugs seemed louder than usual. She could barely hear the stream. Noe wondered if the Smashed Man was there, somewhere around her in Old Man Woods, watching. A bolt of ice shot through her spine as she realized how vulnerable she was alone in the woods and wondered again if the Smashed Man had a whole new set of rules now that he was free.

The darkwash Amberonk sparkled on the rock, as fresh as if it had been painted that morning. A protection sigil, Fern had called it. How did it protect? Who did it protect? Did it even work? The Elberex hadn't worked. Twice now.

The crunch of leaves and sticks startled her enough that she yelled and jumped almost clear to the top of Rune Rock. It was the other Dread Enders. They all looked awful, as awful as Noe assumed she herself looked after a night of sleep deprivation and a morning of terror and worry.

"What happened?" asked Radiah right away.

Noe shook her head. "I painted the Elberex on his forehead and it seemed to work at first. He looked like he was in pain. But then he grabbed me." She pulled back her sleeve to show a dark ring of bruises around her left wrist.

Crystal gasped.

"Did he hurt you?" asked Ruthy.

"I don't think so." The feeling had come back into her arm, but the bruise throbbed still.

"What's wrong with your other hand?" asked Crystal.

She looked down at her right hand, the one that she

had coated in darkwash. Stains covered it like she had a skin disease. She explained about dropping the paintbrush and breaking the vial.

"While he was holding my wrist, I fought him with more of the darkwash. It seemed to hurt him. It helped me get away from him. But then he came all the way out of the wall. Stood up on the floor of my basement. I ran. He . . . didn't chase me." She almost got angry explaining it. Like it wasn't fair that she had to both experience it and explain it.

"Why didn't he chase you after he got out of the wall?" asked Radiah, almost like she wished he had.

"I think because dawn came," said Noe. "But I also wonder how weak he is. It took more than a month for him to recover from Erica's encounter with him. And we had him going in and out of the crack all night. He must be hiding somewhere, recuperating."

"Maybe he's still in your house," said Ruthy.

Noe had already shocked herself with that thought. "He could be," she replied, almost defensively. "But why would he stay so close to the place he's been trying to escape for decades? Especially when a flat monster can hide anywhere." They all looked uncertainly at the base of Rune Rock.

"Maybe he's back in the crack?" said Crystal weakly.

"I knew this was a stupid idea," said Radiah, her eyes livid and her voice raised so loud it drowned out the bugs. "Now we're not safe anywhere. All because you had to take charge. We were fine before. We would have made it through this eventually. He was stuck in our basements. Now he's . . ." She gestured around the forest, trying to find the right words. "You've been here for a month, and you thought you knew everything. And now it's all hopeless."

"Stop it, Radiah!" They all looked in astonishment at Crystal, who had lifted her head and was staring at Radiah with a tearstained face. "Noe was trying to help us. And she had to anyway. You know that. The sleepwalking. We didn't have any other choice."

Radiah looked at Crystal coldly. Then at Noe. She stormed off back to the path. Ruthy gazed sadly after her but stayed in place.

"Maybe this is a good thing," said Ruthy. "Maybe he left the entire neighborhood. Maybe he's gone forever."

"Maybe," Noe said. Maybe he did just want to escape. Maybe he was somebody else's problem now. Was she fine with that? Although it made her feel guilty, she kind of was. They stood in the forest, listening to the summer bugs. There were a lot of maybes in this conversation.

Crystal started to say something but stopped herself.

She took Ruthy by the hand and headed out of the forest. She didn't look back to see if Noe was following.

Noe wasn't following. Noe climbed up on Rune Rock and sat there for another hour, crying and looking through blurry eyes at the Amberonk and the stains on her hand, stains that her parents couldn't see. She had tried to wash it all off, but the darkwash had only faded to a pencil-lead gray. Still, it was enough that her parents' eyes wouldn't turn purple anymore when they saw her hand. She thought about the Elberex. How ludicrous it had felt painting it on the Smashed Man's forehead. The fight should have been more violent. More satisfying, even if she did lose it. Like hitting him with a bat. Not painting on his face like she was a beautician. So stupid.

Eventually she walked home, shut herself in her room, and threw herself on her bed. She was still exhausted. In every way exhausted. So exhausted that she didn't care if the Smashed Man came and got her right now. In her sleep would be best anyway. She thought of the line from Crystal's poem: *smother you in your sleep like a deadly, grinning blanket.* That was fine. She was fine with that. She fell asleep.

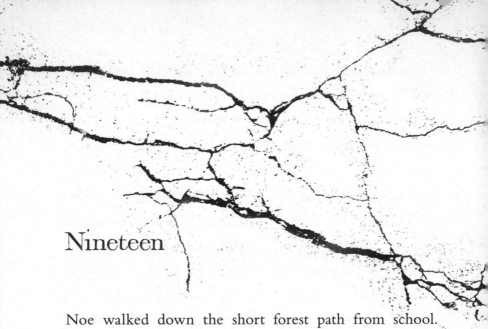

# Nineteen

Noe walked down the short forest path from school. Autumn had taken over the trees, and the colors were everything she'd hoped they'd be in the new neighborhood: red maple and yellow birch and every shade of autumn in between. She hit the asphalt bulb of Totter Court not five minutes after exiting the glass doors of the school. She loved having the school so close to her house. The green metal Pilgrim weather vane squeaked and wobbled between the north and northwest as she crossed the slight hill of her lawn to the front door with its golden autumn wreath stark against the black wood.

The door was unlocked. She walked inside, slipping her backpack into the crook of her left arm. "Mom? Dad?"

"We're in here, Noe!" came Mom's voice from the living room.

170

Noe threw her backpack onto the floor of the front closet—even though she knew Mom would be upset that she didn't hang it on a hook—and turned the corner into the living room.

Noe screamed. Screamed and screamed and screamed.

Her whole family was in the living room. Mom was in the recliner with Len on her lap. They were feeding each other Goldfish crackers and laughing. Dad was lying on his back on the couch, looking at his phone, laughing at something on the screen.

And in the wooden rocking chair, the one that nobody ever sat in because it was more a decorative piece than a functional chair, sat the Smashed Man.

He was folded into a parody of a person sitting. As if somebody had taken a life-sized cardboard cutout of a man, bent the cardboard at the waist and knees, and put it in the chair. The Smashed Man's ghastly frozen smile split his mutilated face. He leered at Mom and Len and then he turned to leer at Dad and then turned back to leer at Mom and Len again.

Eventually, he leered at Noe.

Noe screamed and screamed and screamed until her entire body was shaking with the screams and then she was just shaking and then she realized she was being shaken by somebody else, somebody who was yelling in her ear and

171

then the living room and Mom and Dad and Len and the Smashed Man all disappeared into darkness.

And she was in her bed and the darkness was her room and Dad was shaking her and Mom was yelling, "Noe, you're having a night terror. You're having a night terror, Noe. You're okay. Wake up, honey."

Slowly Noe slipped back into reality. She huffed huge sobs and sank into Dad's chest.

"I'm sorry, Noe. We normally wouldn't wake you up. But this felt like a bad one," said Mom.

"Another bad one," agreed Dad.

🐾 He was referring to the previous night. The night she had released the Smashed Man into the world. They had dismissed her raving and panic as night terrors. Although it was slightly more worrisome than that, because she had, quite literally, dragged Len into it.

"Do you remember what you dreamed?" asked Mom.

"No," said Noe. She didn't want to describe it to them.

"Werewolves?" The question came from the doorway. Len stood there with a stuffed mongoose under one arm and a look of concern on her face.

"Nore, you should go to bed," said Dad. "Noe will be all right." Nobody corrected his nickname for Len.

"No, not werewolves," said Noe, trying her hardest to smile at her sister.

"Hmm," Len said, as if she had drawn insights about her sister from the answer.

"Hey," said Dad, his tone changing from calm-my-daughter-down to change-the-subject-to-something-distracting. "Did we tell you guys we're having a bonfire?"

"What's a bonfire?" asked Len.

"It's a giant fire that you make outside at night."

"At night?" asked Len doubtfully.

"Yes, but it makes a lot of light. You can roast marshmallows on it and hang out with friends around it. It's a lot of fun. What's-her-name, the woman down the street . . ."

"Mrs. Washington," said Mom.

"Right, her. She told us that the neighborhood does one every season to clean up all the forest bits that fall into our lawns. The family that lived in this house before us used to host it. That's what that big ring of rocks out back is for. She asked if we wanted to keep the tradition going, and I said that we'd do it. Sounds like fun, right?"

"Yeah," said Noe.

"At night?" asked Len.

"You'll like it. You'll see," said Dad. "Now let's all get back to bed. Unlike you two, Mom and I don't get to sleep in during the summer."

"Can Len sleep in bed with me?"

"Sure," said Mom. "You want to do that, Len?"

"Yeah!" said Len in the same tone of excitement she used when she was given candy or iPad time.

She jumped into Len's bed with her mongoose, and they snuggled into the pillows and blankets together. Noe stroked her little sister's hair until Len fell asleep. By habit, she reached for the scrunchie in her drawer, but then realized it didn't matter anymore.

She hadn't done much that day. Napped and waited until the windows darkened. Waited for the Smashed Man to come out. "Maybe he's still in your house," Ruthy had said. In one way, Noe did wish that was true. She hoped he was back in the basement wall or outside the universe or wherever he was from. That the Smashed Man wasn't free. That even though he had left the crack, he still had to start over again like when you lose all your lives in a video game. That would make her so happy. It would make the Smashed Man not a threat anymore. Just a loop. Like a ghost walking the same old hallway in the same old castle every night. Noe even fantasized about selling tickets to the kids at school to see him slow-jack-in-the-box his way out, and then make everybody leave, and like a magic trick, return to see him back where he started.

But when she went down that night, he didn't unspool from the crack. It was just an empty crevice in a creepy basement. Like the first time she had seen it. Before her entire life had changed.

But lying there with Len, she realized that just because the Smashed Man had escaped, just because the plan hadn't worked, that didn't change one very important thing. She couldn't let the Smashed Man get Len.

She needed to talk to Fern. She would go to the white house first thing tomorrow.

If she didn't get smothered in the night.

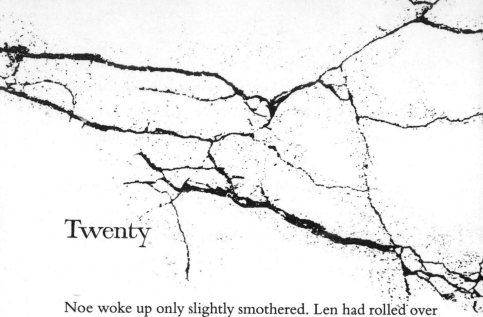

# Twenty

Noe woke up only slightly smothered. Len had rolled over onto her at some point, so she had a three-year-old on her stomach and a mongoose in her face. She gently extricated herself from her two bedfellows and jumped in the shower. She spent most of the time in there scrubbing extra hard at her darkened hand, but the remnants of the darkwash stayed. She threw on some clothes, grabbed Erica's diary—which the girls had let her hold on to for the time being so that she could study it—and headed out to see a woman in an invisible house.

She looked around the neighborhood to make sure nobody was out, walked up to the door beside the Nonatuke, and knocked hard.

No answer. She knocked again and then tried to look like she was just hanging out instead of waiting for an invisible door to open, in case anybody on the block happened to peek out their window. Finally she heard a voice on the other side of the door. "Go away, girl."

"I let the Smashed Man out," Noe said softly.

The door opened. Fern's hair was messy, and she was wearing a red bathrobe that matched her eyeglasses. "You did what?"

"The Smashed Man escaped from my basement. Can I come inside? It looks like I'm talking to an imaginary friend." Fern didn't move, so neither did Noe. Finally Fern retreated back into the house, leaving the front door open. Noe followed her.

Inside it smelled bad. Like sweaty meat. And the mess seemed to have multiplied. Every horizontal surface was being used as a table for clutter, and the laundry piles on the floor were growing like Fern was watering them. She seemed to be taking her dissatisfaction with being here out on the house itself.

Fern leaned on her crutch with one hand and cleared a place on the couch with the other. "Sit," she said, nodding at it before disappearing into the kitchen. She returned with a pot of tea and a single elephant cup on a tray, balanced in one hand just like last time. She set the tray on a box and sat down, laying her crutch on the floor. After pouring herself some chai, she leaned back.

Noe eyed the cup, remembering the sweet, spicy tea and wishing for some. Even if it was served in a disgusting place like this. Fern saw Noe's look and lowered her cup with a sigh. "Go get yourself a cup, I guess. But be careful with it."

Noe tried not to look too eager as she got up and walked into the kitchen. It was as much of a mess as the rest of the house, but it wasn't hard to find one of the elephant teacups in the sink. There was no reason the woman couldn't have brought out two cups herself. Noe washed it out and then walked slowly back into the room. As she poured herself some chai, Fern asked, "Why can you see past the Nonatuke?"

The question surprised Noe enough that she answered honestly. "I have parasomnia."

Fern's eyebrows almost jumped out of the frames of her large red-tinted glasses. "I assume you sleepwalk. Do you have sleep paralysis? Do you talk in your sleep?"

"I sleepwalk and I have night terrors. That's it. That's enough. I hate it."

"Why?"

"Because it ruins my life," said Noe. That was all the explanation she was going to give this woman.

"Do you know what the word 'parasomnia' means?"

"Weird sleep."

"No, that's ignorant. 'Para' doesn't mean weird. It

means 'beyond.' You have an ability that goes beyond sleep."

"It's not an ability. And it's the reason the Smashed Man is out right now." And then Noe talked. She told the surly stranger every detail. Len's sleepwalking. Erica's diary full of unreadable miscolored darkwash she'd found behind the dryer. The purple snake in her dreams. The plan. The pilfered vial of darkwash. She felt exhausted by the time she was finished, and she had gone through three cups of chai.

Fern hadn't gotten through one. She stared into her teacup the entire time, like she was looking for a message in it. When Noe was done, Fern didn't look up. Didn't say anything. She waited a few seconds to make sure Noe wasn't going to say anything else, and then said, "You're a foolish girl."

"You're a jerk adult."

Fern's face froze, and she barely moved her lips as she said, "Yes, but only one of us let a monster into our world."

Noe dropped her head and sank deeper into the couch.

"You haven't seen the Smashed Man since he escaped?" asked Fern.

"No. I mean, it's only been one night since he got out, but none of us saw him last night. Do you think he's . . . gone for good?"

Fern scratched at her ear and stared into her tea, still

waiting for that message. Finally she shook her head. "No. The Smashed Man will try to leave the neighborhood. That's definite. He probably tried last night, in fact. But the Amberonks will keep him here."

"The protection sigils? That's what they're for?"

"They form a border around this neighborhood. For this specific reason. He might be free from the space between here and the stuck place, but he's still trapped here."

A thought entered Noe's head. A disgusting, despicable thought. Fern read it immediately somehow. "Don't think that you can remove the Amberonks, girl. You only know about two of them, but they're in dozens of places, layered so that you'd have to remove half a dozen or so to make a single gap in the border. Even if you could figure out how to remove them." She nodded her head at Noe's discolored hand. "We can't let the Smashed Man into the world. We can't let him be somebody else's problem."

Noe looked down at her empty teacup. "I know, I know. But what about us? What about the people who live here? What do we do?"

"I don't know." Fern thought for a few seconds. "Tell me again about touching the Smashed Man with the dark-wash."

"It didn't hurt like when I touched him with my bare

hand. I guess the darkwash protected me. I just felt stupid doing it. Like I was doing it wrong. I wanted it to feel like I was attacking him, not painting him."

"And this plan was based on a snake that turned into an Elberex in this girl Erica's dream?"

"And the snake in mine. Except they were two different snakes."

"Two different snakes." Fern pondered the phrase in silence. Noe took the opportunity to pour more chai, but the teapot was empty.

"Can the Neighbors help?" asked Noe.

"No." Fern abruptly dropped her teacup on the tray with a loud clank. "Unfortunately for me, I think the answer to the Smashed Man is going to come from you."

"What do you mean? I've already messed up once trying to get rid of him."

"The Neighbors don't know much about the stuck places, but how do you think we know what we know?"

Noe shrugged her shoulders.

"Think about it with more than your shoulders, girl. We can't sense them. Science books don't talk about them. It's not on the internet. How do you think the Neighbors know what we know?"

"Shrug," said Noe.

Fern lifted her glasses and rubbed one of her eyes.

"There's one body of knowledge that we can all access: our bodies. Every single one of us is a library. The human body has about a hundred trillion cells. Each cell contains one point five gigabytes of information. That means you, Noelle Wiley, represent a hundred and fifty trillion gigs of information. You are a walking internet."

"That makes no sense."

"Of course it does. We're made of ancient stuff. The subatomic particles of our bodies have been around since the universe began. But aside from the cosmic stuff, your body knows a lot. How to pump blood, how to digest food, how to keep us alive. Cells know how to replicate, your immune system, how to repel sickness. We have instincts for avoiding danger. We didn't need to learn any of that, because it was already there."

"You mean we can trust our guts?" That was a phrase she'd heard Mom say once. At the time, Noe had just thought it was a disgusting phrase. Like cul-de-sac.

"Quite literally. Because the materials we are made of have always been around in one form or another, at the center of stars, in comets, in the dirt we walk on, as part of past civilizations, and they are constantly gathering information. So there's a lot of information to be had, if we know how to access it." For a moment, Fern sounded more awestruck than grumpy. "And that's how we learned

182

about stuck places and what the sigils are, and what they do—or, at least, what two of them do. All that knowledge came from inside somebody. Cell knowledge, we call it. That's why you and that other girl were so confident about using the Elberex on the Smashed Man. You knew it in your guts."

"But we were both wrong," said Noe.

"You only had some of the information you needed. You can put a bunch of facts together and still come to the wrong conclusion. Accessing cell knowledge is difficult and not at all reliable. That's why the Neighbors are so ignorant."

"You think the answer to defeating the Smashed Man is . . . inside me?"

"Maybe. I think your snake dreams were you accessing that cell knowledge. I think your parasomnia helps you access it. Or maybe the knowledge caused the parasomnia. Either way, you need to go deeper." Fern put her teacup down and stared at the ceiling. After a few seconds of silence, she sighed. "I can show you how to go deeper. But only because it could be valuable for the Neighbors. Don't think for a second that I'm getting involved for any other reason."

She grabbed her crutch and levered herself out of the camp chair with it. She waded through the detritus covering the floor to a corner of the room. She pushed a pile of empty boxes out of the way with her free hand, smashing a pair of beakers in the process. It sounded to Noe like when she had smashed the vial of darkwash against the water heater.

Noe didn't question her. She put down her empty teacup and followed Fern to the corner. Noe would try anything to get rid of the Smashed Man. Especially now that she had unleashed it on the neighborhood.

"Sit here in the corner. Face the wall."

Noe gingerly moved some of the splinters of glass out of the way and sat cross-legged, facing the corner.

"Close your eyes and think about the Elberex. Think about the Smashed Man. Think about the purple snake from your nightmares. Keep your eyes shut. Don't think about little girl things. Focus." Noe settled deeper into the dirty carpet and squeezed her eyelids shut. "I'm going to give you something to repeat. A mantra to help you focus. Om."

"Um," tried Noe.

"No, no. Om. O-m. Rhymes with 'home.' But I want you to say it like this . . ." Fern drew the syllable out for five seconds, like she was humming it.

"Is om one of the sigils?"

"No. It's Hindu. A mystical syllable. Some say it's the

184

sound that started the universe. And that's what you're trying to access. Ancient knowledge. Sun heart knowledge.
Cell knowledge. Gut knowledge. It will help you focus if
you repeat it over and over. If you do it right, you won't
even know you're saying it."

Noe started repeating it. It felt silly. "Is this meditating?" she asked so that she could take a break from the
mantra.

"Similar."

Noe heard the clank of Fern's crutch moving away,
heard her sorting carelessly through a pile of things, heard
some of those things breaking, heard her say something
angry that she couldn't make out, and then Noe heard her
breathing behind her and the loud ticking of what sounded
like a clock. "I've placed a metronome on the floor behind
you. Do you know what a metronome is?" Noe shook
her head. "It's a device for keeping time. Musicians use it.
Hypnotists use it. Time your oms with the rhythm of the
clicks. Think about the purple snake."

She imagined the Neighbors sitting cross-legged in
a room with their eyes closed, singing "om" over and
over again, trying to learn the secrets of all the universes
whizzing past them. No wonder they didn't know much.
Still, she repeated the mantra. And repeated the mantra. And repeated the mantra. "I don't think this is . . . ,"

started Noe, but Fern shushed her.

"No talking. Only om."

Noe started again. She concentrated on the snake and the Elberex. The crack in her basement wall. She couldn't bring herself to focus on the Smashed Man himself, though. While she thought about those things, she chanted. Eventually, after what seemed like a long time, as the metronome clicked away behind her, it became relaxing, and she felt herself loosen, like she was becoming untethered from herself, a kite on a broken string.

And then she felt a night terror coming on. The meditation must have relaxed her into falling asleep. She was in a dark space, floating, surrounded by the purple snake. The eyeless creature was swimming in a big loop around her. Slowly, like it was gradually freezing in place. Eventually it broke the loop and headed right for her in that same slow motion. Like it was taking hours.

Suddenly, she felt hot, very hot, uncomfortably hot. That had never happened in her nightmare before. Soon the purple snake started jerking in the hot, dark space as it floated toward her. The jerking turned into longer motions as the snake twisted back on itself, its head touching its tail to form the two loops of an Elberex. The purple Elberex hardened in front of her. That was the only way she could describe it. The Elberex now looked more like an inanimate object than a snake, but it floated slowly toward her in space like the snake had. As the sigil came closer, the heat increased. And right when she thought the sigil would sear itself painfully into her face, she was back behind her eyelids. Back in the corner. Back in the white house. She could hear the metronome clicking away.

"I fell asleep," she said, stretching her arms and arching her back.

"No, you didn't," said Fern. She seemed far away.

"What happened, then?"

"I would say that you have a natural talent for accessing cell knowledge," said Fern. "Makes sense that it would be easier for a sleepwalker."

"How long has it been?"

"Two hours," said Fern.

Noe pulled herself quickly to her feet, upsetting a small metal box on the floor with a strip of metal on it that swung back and forth like an upside-down pendulum. That must have been the metronome. "That's not true." She slid her phone out of her pocket and glanced at the time. It had been two hours.

Fern was sitting in the camp chair. She had changed from her red robe to jeans and a green-and-blue paisley blouse. She held a sandwich in one hand, leafy green lettuce and red tomatoes peeking out from around rye bread, and she was flipping through Erica's diary with the other. Noe didn't like seeing Fern holding the book, much less reading it. Even though what Erica had written wasn't that private. Even though it was important information Fern needed to see. "What did your cells tell you?" Fern asked.

"I don't know, but I had the same nightmare—the purple snake. Although the nightmare went longer this time. More happened. The snake turned into an Elberex, like Erica said. But it wasn't made of darkwash. It was purple. And it was solid, like metal or stone."

"Solid? Anything else different?"

Noe tried to imagine herself back in the dark space. "Right before the snake turned into the Elberex, everything got hot. Like really hot. I thought the Elberex was going to burn me."

Suddenly Fern dropped her sandwich onto the nearest stack of books, along with Erica's diary. She got up with her crutch and started rooting in the piles of clothes around her. "Where's my duffel bag? Do you see it? It's black with red straps . . . oh, there it is."

"What do you need a duffel bag for?"

"To pack it for a trip. What do you do with duffel bags?"

"Where are you going? What about the meditation? What about the Smashed Man?"

Fern was bending over her crutch and throwing things into a black duffel bag. Clothes, books, vials. Her elephant teapot. Her lettuce-and-tomato sandwich. "I think I know the fastest way to get me back to Gulf Shores. Maybe even push the science of stuck places forward half a step. I've got to get the Neighbors in on this, though. Now."

"Where are they?"

"Not here."

"When are you coming back?"

"Don't know. Days, weeks, months?" Fern rushed through the kitchen. Noe followed her, confused. Fern opened a door that led to the garage. In it was an ancient Volkswagen Beetle. The car was bright orange and looked like a toy.

"What are we supposed to do about the Smashed Man?" asked Noe.

"I don't know. Stay near adults? You probably know better than I do." Fern slipped into the car, throwing the duffel bag and her crutch on the passenger seat. She turned the keys, and the car rumbled like it was about to fly apart. She then pointed a finger at Noe, like she was lecturing her from inside the car. Noe looked around and saw a switch on the wall beside her. She hit it. The garage door opened with a metal wail. Fern sped backward out of the garage.

She didn't make it to the end of the driveway before

she pulled back in as fast as she had left. She leaned across the front seat and rolled the window down with a lot of effort. "Here," she said, holding out a small metal key. Noe took it. "To this house. Don't clean my mess up." She sat back in the driver seat. "Nighttime is the most dangerous for you. That's still going to be when the Smashed Man is active." And with that she was off again.

Noe didn't see a Nonatuke on the car and wondered if anybody saw the funny-looking vehicle appear out of thin air at the top of the dead end. But the thought was dashed quickly from her head as reality set in. The Smashed Man was trapped in this neighborhood and there was no way to fight him and it was all her fault. Fern had been her only hope, and now she was gone who knows where for who knows how long. Fern hadn't been helping her today, she'd been using her. Using her for her . . . cell knowledge. If that was even a real thing. Noe had her doubts.

She sat down in Fern's dirty kitchen and cried. After about ten minutes of wringing herself dry, she rooted around the kitchen, looking for tissues or napkins or paper towels. But instead she found something that made her realize that there might be a way for the Dread Enders to protect themselves.

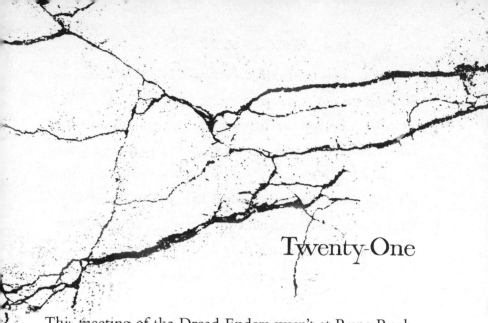

# Twenty-One

This meeting of the Dread Enders wasn't at Rune Rock. It was in Noe's bedroom. Her palace of parasomnia, the starting line of her sleepwalking and the headquarters of her night terrors. It felt weird having them all in there, Radiah messing with her phone while sitting on Noe's bed, Crystal looking at the posters of dogs on her walls, Ruthy playing with a stuffed Komodo dragon that Len must have left at some point. But it also felt good. She had just finished explaining to the other girls about her conversation with Fern and the meditation session.

"So, again, she's no help at all," said Radiah. It had been awkward seeing Radiah after their last encounter, but she seemed to have cooled a bit. She must have talked to Crystal since then. Or maybe it was the threat of the Smashed Man. They were all bonded by terror.

"Yeah, she's awful. But she was a little help," said Noe. "Even if she didn't mean to be."

"What do you mean?" asked Crystal, almost too quietly to hear. It was the first time she'd said anything since arriving. She was staring at a perplexing poster of a puli, a Hungarian breed that looked like a living mop. Crystal had been strangely silent since arriving at Noe's house, choosing to be interested only in the posters so far.

"She told us about the Amberonks. And she has these." Noe held up a vial of darkwash.

"Not again," said Radiah.

"I know, I know. But this isn't for offense anymore. It's for defense. Fern said that the Amberonks keep the Smashed Man from escaping the neighborhood. That means they can keep the Smashed Man from . . . entering parts of it." Radiah was off her phone, Ruthy had put down the stuffed reptile, and Crystal had stopped staring at the dog posters. She had all their attention now. "If we painted darkwash Amberonks on our houses, he won't be able to get inside."

"Unless he's already inside one of our houses," said Radiah.

"Fern said he's trying to escape the neighborhood. So he must be out there trying to find a way through the Amberonks," said Noe. "But if he is, we'll just have to lure him out. And then he won't be able to get back in."

"Do you really think it'll work?" asked Ruthy.

"I think so. We'd have to paint them on all four sides of our houses to make like a mini border around them," said Noe.

"What about the roof?" said Radiah, her tone shifting. "Don't we need to put one on the roof to keep him from getting in that way?"

It seemed like a weird thing to say until Noe remembered that the girl lived in an attic. "He can't get over the Amberonks painted around the neighborhood, so he shouldn't be able to get over the Amberonks painted around a house."

"Since adults can't see the darkwash, it should be easy to do," said Radiah. "We'll need a lot more than that, though." She nodded her head at the small vial in Noe's hand.


It's hard to ransack a house that already looks like it's been ransacked. Digging through all the old food and clothes and books and dirty glassware in the white house was disgusting, but it was harder trying to keep track of where they had already looked. Most of the mess in the house was on the first floor. Upstairs were empty rooms and a bedroom where Fern must have slept. There wasn't much up there.

"What've we got?" Noe asked as they all stood in the living room.

"Five vials," said Crystal, pushing them around on the brass tea tray. "Two of them only half full." She stared at the vials like she didn't want to look anybody in the eyes.

"How big do we need to paint the sigils?" asked Ruthy. "Can we make them small?"

"The smallest one we've seen is on the Dead End sign. I'm guessing the Amberonks will have to be at least that size," said Noe. "But to be sure, we should make them bigger than that."

Radiah was over by a door at the side of the living room. She touched the knob uncertainly and then opened the door a few inches and peered in. "Did anybody look in the basement?"

The basement of the white house didn't look like it belonged in the white house. It was clean. It also didn't look like it belonged in any house. It was a laboratory. The floor was tiled, and pristine white counters ran the length of one wall. On their surfaces were microscopes and other scientific apparatuses. Glass beakers and vials were arranged in orderly cabinets. Three whiteboards on wheels clustered together in one corner, covered in numbers and sigils. Cameras stood on tall tripods beside mounted studio lights. Noe rethought her image of the Neighbors

194

meditating cross-legged on a floor.

The only part of the basement that seemed like it belonged in the basement was one of the walls. Unlike the spotless white plaster of the other walls, this one was dingy, bare concrete. Nothing was in front of the wall, and every camera and light in the room was pointed at it.

On its surface, covering almost every square inch, was a maze of cracks.

"This is what Fern has been up to," said Radiah.

"Look at this." Crystal held a large black notebook she had found on one of the counters. The girls gathered around her as she opened it. It was the notebook of sigils that Erica had mentioned in her diary.

"Not much help," said Radiah. Noe had to agree. There were a couple dozen symbols in the book, about half of which were named with the same kinds of nonsensical names as Nonatuke and Amberonk. Those two sigils were the only ones with explanations of their purpose, though.

As Crystal flipped through the pages, Noe saw the Elberex flash by. It made her uncomfortable, so she moved away and started digging through cabinets. After rummaging around, she found what she was looking for in a cabinet under the counter. Inside were large lidded white buckets labeled DARKWASH that, judging from their weight, were full of the black starry liquid. "We're going to need bigger paintbrushes. And something to carry one of these around in," she said.

The Dread Enders continued to poke around the laboratory, but there wasn't much more to see: a few blank notebooks. A blocky laptop that looked like the first one ever invented. It was dead and had no power cord. And none of the cameras had memory cards in them. "Can they even record the Smashed Man?" Radiah asked.

It took two of them to lug one of the heavy buckets of darkwash outside to the front lawn. Noe tried to make as little eye contact with the other girls as possible, to avoid seeing their purple irises every time they glanced at where the house was. The group made a quick plan, then left the bucket on the ground and dispersed to their houses.

They met back at the white bucket ten minutes later, ready to graffiti Dread End.

Radiah and Ruthy had raided Ruthy's garage for paintbrushes and a screwdriver. Crystal returned pulling an old wooden wagon behind her. Noe had a sheaf of papers in her hand.

"I guess we should do the white house first," said Noe. "Nobody lives there right now, but we don't want to give the Smashed Man a place to hide." They'd set the bucket inside Crystal's wagon. Noe went over to it and, using the screwdriver, popped off the plastic top. Then she dipped her brush into the paint. She looked up at her purple-eyed friends and said, "I guess I'm on my own on this one."

Noe ran to the front of the house, holding the paintbrush like a melting ice-cream cone. She painted the Amberonk prominently on the red door of the house, equal in size to the Nonatuke beside it on the wall. The darkwash was thick and sticky but transferred easily from the brush to the door. It took only three quick brushstrokes to get it on there. When she turned around, her friends were still looking up at her with purple eyes. She made quick work of dashing back for more darkwash and painting Amberonks on the back and sides of the house.

They went counterclockwise around the neighborhood. Radiah's house was next.

The work was absurdly quick. Four Dread Enders, four paintbrushes, four sides to the house. "That's it?" asked Radiah. "I don't feel safer."

They moved on to Ruthy's witch house next. The darkwash was so deeply black, it made the black paint of her house look faded. On her front door, which was red, the Amberonk looked like an accent to the rest of the house.

They continued down the street, painting Amberonks on the doors and sides of all the houses on Totter Court, creating barriers that the Smashed Man could not break and markings that the adults could not see. They decided to do every house on the block, even though only their own houses had kids in them. Adults couldn't see the Smashed Man and seemed not to be in danger of him when he was in the basement walls, but the Dread Enders didn't know if those rules had changed now that the Smashed Man was free.

All they knew right now was how strange it felt to paint sigils on other people's houses. Like vandalism, but since nobody could see it, pretend vandalism, like Erica throwing a rock through the window of an invisible house.

Fortunately, they only got caught once.

They felt comfortable walking up to front doors and brazenly painting Amberonks on them. That was because the darkwash was invisible, but also because they had a cover story ready if they needed it. The sides and back of the houses were harder and a little trespass-y, but not impossible. Eventually they found themselves at the mouth of the cul-de-sac, where the Dread End sign marked the border of their neighborhood and the cage of the Smashed Man. They worked their way up the other side of the neighborhood toward Noe's house and had just finished Crystal's yellow house. They were moving on to her neighbor, Mrs. Washington. Her husband had passed away years ago, and she lived by herself. The girls hadn't even had a chance to set foot on the walkway to the front door when they heard Mrs. Washington yelling from a wooden swing on her porch.

"What are you girls doing to this neighborhood?"

Crystal sighed and took the lead. Mrs. Washington was her neighbor, after all, and she had talked to Mrs. Washington lots of times before, although mostly just to say hi or to see if she needed help carrying her groceries into the house.

Crystal reached into the wagon and pulled out a piece of paper from a stack there. "Hi, Mrs. Washington," she said flatly as she walked up to the porch. "We're handing out these." She gave Mrs. Washington the piece of paper.

On it, below an image of a bonfire on a beach, were the words:

**You're invited to the summer bonfire!!!**
**The Wileys (6 Totter Court) would like to invite**
**all neigbors to our backyard for the seasonal bonfire**
**to keep our neighborhood clean!!!**

Noe had typed up the flyer, copied and pasted the photo from an image search, and then printed a dozen of them off Dad's printer. It wasn't until after she'd printed them that she realized the bonfire image was on a beach and that she'd mistyped "neighbors." She also couldn't remember the exact date of the bonfire and she hated exclamation marks, but all that didn't matter. It was shoddy work, but it should work if somebody opened the front door when they were trying to paint an Amberonk on it, even if it looked like they were running a dry brush up and down the door.

Mrs. Washington took the flyer, read it, and then shielded her eyes as she looked past Crystal at the two girls by the wagon on the sidewalk.

"Which one of you is a Wiley?" she yelled across the lawn.

Noe raised her hand slowly like she was admitting to doing something wrong. Mrs. Washington squinted her eyes and nodded her head and then found the bucket more interesting than the new girl on the block.

"What's with the white bucket?" she asked.

"It's for pine cones. We're gathering them for an art project. Ruthy's idea." Noe tousled Ruthy's hair like she would do to Len if she wanted a reaction from her. Ruthy took the indignity well.

"Not a lot of pine trees in the neighborhood," said Mrs. Washington. "Best place for those is closer to the edge of the woods, especially behind your house. And what's with all the paintbrushes?"

"We're going to paint the pine cones." Noe twirled her brush in front of her like she was casting a spell with a wand, while watching a small glob of darkwash drip onto the grass in front of her. Mrs. Washington, of course, only saw a dry paintbrush.

Noe was about to go into even more detail about what a bunch of kids with pine cones and paintbrushes would be doing, even if she had no idea what those details would be, when she saw Radiah peeking around the side of the house. Radiah had a paintbrush gloppy with darkwash in one hand and was giving a thumbs-up with the other. They could see the Amberonk she had painted on the front of the house right there at the edge, where Mrs. Washington couldn't see her do it. It was one of four that she had painted on its walls while the rest of the Dread Enders were distracting Mrs. Washington.

"Thanks!" said Noe. "We'll look for pine cones at the edge of the forest after we finish passing out the flyers."

Radiah rejoined them one house later. Five houses later, they were putting the final Amberonk on the side of Noe's house. Noe painted the last one under the kitchen window while she stared defiantly at the black door through the glass. "That's it," she said, turning around. And then she started laughing.

"What?" asked Crystal as they all looked around to try to figure out why Noe was laughing.

"This stuff doesn't come off easy," said Noe, lifting up the hand that was still stained from her confrontation with the Smashed Man. The girls all looked at each other and noticed flecks and streaks of it on their arms and faces and even, in Ruthy's case, in her bright blond hair.

"I think I feel it tingling," said Radiah, looking at a streak of it on her left arm.

Noe kept laughing. "It does that at first. You can scrub it until it fades. Hopefully at some point it goes away. At least no adults can see it."

"We're filthy with this stuff and there's no way our parents will get mad at us," said Crystal, coming out of the strange funk she had been in all day and joining in Noe's laughter. "I wish there were more things they couldn't see."

"Like a pet dog!" shouted Noe.

"Like me on my phone during dinner!" shouted Radiah.

"Like . . . like . . . like," tried Ruthy before stomping her foot and giving up. The girls laughed even harder. For the first time, the Dread Enders felt safe in their own neighborhood. But the laughs finally tittered awkwardly into silence.

"Where do you think he is?" asked Ruthy, looking around at the forest surrounding them.

They all did the same.

"I don't know," said Noe.

"If there's any day to not talk about the Smashed Man, it's today," said Radiah. "You guys want to play some video games at my house?"

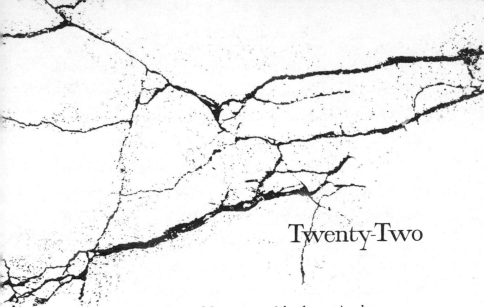

# Twenty-Two

Radiah stood in her old room with the attic door open in front of her. She looked up the stairs at the dimness above. There was only so much a single light bulb could do by itself in such a dark space. She looked around at her old bedroom, where she hadn't slept a single night in three years. The bedding was clean and fresh—her mother kept it that way, hoping it would tempt her down from the mustiness of the attic, not understanding why she wasn't coming down from the attic. But at least her mom let her stay up there.

What Radiah had never told her was that she was tempted every night to come down those stairs and curl up in those sheets. The attic was isolating. Which was why she stayed there. But it was hard. She rarely ever drew anymore.

Maybe tonight she should sleep in her real bedroom.

Radiah looked out the front window at the neighborhood. She could see lights on in Noe's house and the streetlamps on the road, but being surrounded by ravine walls and forest meant that the streetlamps were about as effective as the attic light bulb. Before it got dark, Radiah had walked around the house to make sure all the Amberonks were still there. Noe said they were difficult to wash off, but that didn't mean impossible. All four were there, dark and glittery against the blue siding, and seeming completely inadequate to their task of keeping the Smashed Man away.

She had invited Ruthy to stay over tonight. She had almost invited everyone to stay over, after they had spent a couple of hours playing video games. But for some reason, Radiah hadn't asked everybody. Only Ruthy. But Ruthy had said no. Radiah understood why. Ruthy's first good night's rest in her entire life should be in her own bed in her own house.

And that decided it for her. Radiah shut the closet door and got into the freshly made bed, pulling the clean sheets up around her neck and breathing in their fabric softener scent. She looked at one of the pictures framed on the wall. A large panther on a rock that she had drawn after reading *The Jungle Book*. She hadn't liked the book that much, but she had loved Bagheera. Radiah got back up, sat down at her desk, grabbed a pencil and paper, and started drawing. Drawing like she hadn't drawn in a long while. Drawing with purpose. With passion. Drawing something flat and awful sliding out of a basement wall. Drawing until she had exhausted herself and returned to bed, instantly falling asleep as soon as she hit those clean-laundry sheets.

Tonight was the first night Ruthy felt good about going to bed. Normally, going to bed meant nighttime, and nighttime meant that below, the Smashed Man was waiting in the cracks of her basement.

But now it was out of her basement. Out of her house. And the Amberonks painted on her house were keeping it from coming back inside. Her house was finally safe. Even if the neighborhood wasn't.

It felt so good to live in a safe house that she had turned down Radiah's offer to stay over at her house. Ruthy felt bad about that, but she wanted to stay in her house tonight. In her bed. With nothing in the cracks of her basement.

Ruthy even went to bed early, before it was nighttime, without waiting for her dad to tell her to.

But before she jumped into bed, she had something important to do.

She twirled around the room like a mad dancer, her fingers lobster pincers. She grabbed up paper monsters from the floor, from the dresser, from the top of the toy box. She was a giant monster seizing the residents of a terrified city. She ripped them down from where they were taped to the walls, to the doors, to the bed—the quick, sharp snap of breaking adhesive their short-lived screams of fright.

As she grabbed each gray, flat monster, she crumbled it into a ball and threw it in a wild arc toward a small teal trash can with a white pony on it that sat in the corner of her room. The construction paper balls missed the trash can more often than they landed inside, but that was fine. It gave her the chance to throw the monsters away again.

Eventually she tired of her revenge. She didn't trash all of the Smashed Men, but she got most of them. The trash can was overflowing with wads of dull paper. She picked one of the remaining uncrumpled paper monsters and taped it to the headboard of her bed, above where her head would be if she lay down. She went into the bathroom and brushed her teeth, put on her pajamas, and vaulted onto the bed, which had always been a few inches too tall for her to get into easily. She grabbed the covers in one hand and her penguin in the other and then coiled herself up into a cozy ball.

At the first stillness of her limbs, she fell asleep.

Noe decided to sleep without tying herself to her bedpost. She had done it before, but it was out of apathy. Tonight would be different. She would fully experience the joys of rolling over in bed. She still went through the rest of her nightly rituals, though. She checked on Len, who was asleep in bed with both hands wrapped around a sloth. She checked the baby gate to make sure it was locked shut and then tied with her purple sash. She still didn't want Len wandering around in her sleep. It was dangerous even without a monster in the basement. She spent her usual twenty minutes on her laptop, looking for any scrap of information about the Smashed Man or stuck places or the Neighbors. Nothing, as usual.

The night was hot, and she had opened her window hoping to coax into her room a stray breeze lost from some cooler climate. It wasn't working very well. Noe closed her laptop, which was putting out even more heat, and set it back on the desk, placing it right on top of the black scrunchie that would normally be around her wrist and the bedpost. She reached into the space between her bed and the wall and pulled out Erica's diary. Even though it seemed they had protected themselves from the Smashed Man for the foreseeable future—as long as they didn't go outside at night—that didn't mean everything was fine. They would still have to deal with the Smashed Man at some point.

She scoured the pages of Erica's diary for the hundredth time, looking for some clue that she had missed. Something that explained why Erica's plan hadn't worked. Why her own plan hadn't worked. That would explain the images in her meditation session.

She could try meditating. See if it worked when she was by herself. She didn't have a metronome, but the meditation word was easy enough. Except that the last thing she wanted was her parents or Len to walk in on her cross-legged in a corner, humming strange sounds. Not that they hadn't seen more embarrassing things from her when she sleepwalked.

A noise came from her window. A scratching at the edge of the forest. An animal. A fox or a fisher or maybe a deer. She'd been hearing noises outside her window ever since they moved next to this forest, but she hadn't worried too much about them, because whatever was making those noises was far below her second-story window. She was as safe from those noises right now as she was from great white sharks out in the ocean.

But now the sound could be from the Smashed Man. Did he walk? Float? Did he slither through the leaves like a snake? The noise sounded like slithering. Loud slithering. Like a very big snake. The image of the Smashed Man slithering up the side of the house and into her open window popped into her head. A chill spread across her skin, not at all like the cool breeze she wanted.

Even though the Amberonk on that side of the house protected her, Noe still got up and shut the window.

Back in bed, another image jumped into her brain, this one of her sleepwalking downstairs and out the front door, only to run into the Smashed Man rearing up from the ground in front of her.

She lifted her laptop, retrieved the scrunchie, and tied her wrist to the bedpost.

Len lay in bed with her eyes closed and the blanket covering most of her face, waiting for Noe to check on her like she did every night. Noe always did the same thing. She fussed with the baby gate and then peeked into Len's room. Len would watch her while she was in the hallway, but then quickly shut her eyes when Noe looked in.

Tonight she was holding Slothie. Len could feel his soft fur against her face and see the dark dots of his eyes and nose in the light from her unicorn lamp. Choosing Slothie had been a hard decision. She had thought about Aardie, her aardvark, or Cappie, her capybara, but she'd realized it had been a long time since she'd slept with Slothie and she needed to be fair, even though Noe told her all the time that life wasn't fair. Len was still willing to give life the benefit of the doubt. So she had plucked the tree mammal from her pile of animal friends in the corner of her bed and held on to it while she pretended to be asleep for Noe.

Noe had been acting strange since they moved to the new house. But that made sense to Len. This house was strange. The whole neighborhood was strange. At first she thought it was the werewolves in the basement. Noe was definitely terrified of the basement. So was Len. Back at their old house, Len had thought werewolves were everywhere. In her closet. Under her bed. Outside the windows. But in this house, it was definitely in the basement.

Werewolves in the basement. Len gripped Slothie tighter and fell immediately to sleep.

Crystal lay in her bed in the dark, staring at the ceiling and crying softly. Even though she was safe at home, a set of Amberonks surrounding her house, the Smashed Man was still out there, roaming the neighborhood. And it was her fault. She had let her friends down. Worse, she had put them all in danger.

Noe's plan had sounded solid. It was the type of plan Erica would have approved of. It technically *was* Erica's plan. But Crystal couldn't do her part.

She couldn't stand there in her basement, in her schoolroom, and face him, making him come out of the wall until the last possible second. Instead, after that first time when she had barely stayed long enough for him to get just his head out of the wall, she had not gone down at all. She had stayed upstairs and faked it with text messages. That meant she had given the Smashed Man rest periods throughout the night. She hadn't merely ruined Noe's plan. She had sabotaged it.

And now the Smashed Man was free.

None of the other Dread Enders had a problem with their part in the plan. Noe, who was brand-new to the horrors of Totter Court, did it. Radiah did it. Even Ruthy did it, although Radiah was by her side. Except that the way Radiah told it, Ruthy was the braver one that night. She was certainly braver than Crystal had been.

Everything was okay for the time being, but they couldn't hide from the Smashed Man forever. Crystal cried until she fell asleep.

The Smashed Man slid silently out from the back of the refrigerator, his flat body upright and clinging to the wall like a tapestry. He followed the wall around the corner, never losing contact, until he reached the staircase. At the foot of the staircase, he bent over from the top of his head, forming an arch and lowering his head and arms onto the steps. He slithered up the stairs like a flat snake, and as quick as one. At the top of the stairs, he rose upward to his full height and walked down the middle of the hall, slow and uncertain, like a three-dimensional person walks underwater.

His gait was actually less a walk and more a wobble, his legs and torso wavering with the repeated impacts of each fall of his flat feet on the carpet. He held his arms out in front of him, rippling in the air, a nightmare walking through physics that didn't make sense. But this wasn't a nightmare. This was the real hallway of a real house in the real world.

Grayish rags wrapped around the arms and legs of the Smashed Man, and the psychotic glee on his face was unchanging. He continued down the darkened hallway until he reached a closed door. He stopped and wavered for a moment, seeming to detect something on the other side of it. He again bent into an arch like an inchworm, feeding the top of his body under the crack beneath the door and sliding through.

On the other side of the door, he stood up. His two-dimensional head twisted on his two-dimensional neck as he surveyed the darkened room. Finally he stepped back against the wall, sliding across it and behind a dresser. Staying close to the wall, he slid out again until he was behind a headboard. From there, the Smashed Man slid feetfirst under the bed until he reached the other end. He slowly unfurled himself.

A girl nestled in the covers and pillows.

He floated the top of his body across the girl until his hideous face was inches above hers. She opened her eyes. She didn't scream, didn't move.

The Smashed Man dropped down on top of her in the darkness.

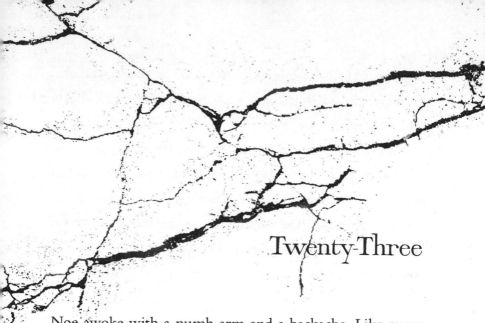

# Twenty-Three

Noe awoke with a numb arm and a backache. Like every morning. Without opening her eyes, she reached up with her working hand and untied the black scrunchie shackling her to the bedpost. The arm dropped to her side and she lay there waiting for the million-sharp-teeth pain of all the blood flowing back into it. When it did, she bit her lip until it subsided. She opened her eyes, registering things slowly. Daylight through the windows. Her closet door open. Len's stuffed Komodo dragon on the floor. Her phone beaming 100% charged from its dock, and the time: 8:07 a.m. All the usual things about her room in the morning. Except that something seemed off.

She got up and wiggled into a T-shirt and jeans. She ran her tongue over her teeth and weighed whether she needed to brush or not. She needed to but decided on not.

She walked into the hallway and saw that the baby gate

213

was open, the robe sash lying on the floor. She looked into her sister's room, but it was a plush zoo without its sticky, tiny zookeeper.

She walked down the hall to her parents' room. The door was open, the bed unmade. And then Noe realized why things didn't seem usual. It was quiet. Len should be running around talking loudly to her animals. Her parents should be getting ready for work. The smell of breakfast should be greeting her. There should be some activity in the house at this time in the morning. It felt like the time she had gotten up and ready for school only to learn that it had been canceled because of snow and everyone was still in bed.

As she started down the stairs, she saw that the front door was also open. That plus the quiet made her wonder if she was experiencing a night terror. If so, she'd walk out that door to see . . . something scary. It could be anything. The Smashed Man had a lot to contend with in her nightmares. But if she was this self-aware, it couldn't be a night terror. Still, it felt as if she was moving slowly, like the air had turned to cotton around her, like she would never make it through that front door.

But then something came through from the outside.

Mom and Len.

Mom was disheveled, like she had just gotten out of

bed. Her robe was wrapped around her and she was wearing slippers. Len was still in her pajamas and hugging a sloth to her chest. Mom saw Noe on the stairs but didn't say anything to her. "Len, go sit down in the kitchen, and I'll pour you some cereal." After throwing a quick look at Noe, Len obeyed.

"What's wrong? Where's Dad?" asked Noe.

"He's across the street. Something happened last night."

Noe's heart dropped so hard she thumped to a seated position on the stairs. "What happened?"

"One of the girls in the neighborhood won't wake up. They're taking her to the hospital." Mom bit at one of her knuckles in a way that Noe had never seen her do before.

Noe sat there stunned, and didn't follow Mom into the kitchen for breakfast. Instead, she walked slowly outside, still feeling like she was wrapped in cotton. Outside, she saw a commotion of ambulances and police cars and people across the street in front of Ruthy's and Radiah's houses. She could see the Amberonk on Radiah's door. It was still there. So was the one on Ruthy's. The sigil was supposed to protect them all in the night.

Noe saw Dad with a small knot of people by one of the ambulances. The only other person she recognized was Mrs. Washington. Noe wavered between running across the road and waiting for Dad to come back. Eventually, after what seemed like hours, Dad left the group and slowly returned to the house. He looked haggard, his hair sticking up in the back and his clothes looking like he'd thrown on the first things his hands had touched in the dirty clothes bin. He saw Noe and gave her a weak smile.

"Who is it?" Noe asked when he had gotten close enough.

"The Larson girl. Ruthy."

If her heart had dropped before, this felt like a punch in the space where it had been. Her eyes filled and she gazed around at the blurring neighborhood, half expecting Crystal and Radiah to be standing in the middle of the street with angry looks of blame on their faces.

Noe knew where she needed to go, but she wasn't ready yet. She went back inside and shambled upstairs. She brushed her teeth for a very long time. She changed into a different T-shirt and a different pair of jeans. She checked behind her bed to make sure Erica's diary was still there. She moved the Komodo dragon back to Len's room. She picked up the robe sash from the hallway floor and put it in her room. She tried new search terms online to see if anybody had ever posted anything similar to their situation—"mysterious coma" was one term, "Eye of Horus" was another—but didn't find any relevant results.

She didn't message Radiah or Crystal. Didn't receive

any from them, either. After putting off leaving for too long, she walked out the back door, across the yard, and into Old Man Woods like an exorcised ghost.

Radiah and Crystal were already at Rune Rock. Both perched atop it, holding each other. Their faces were swollen and blotchy.

"What happened?" was all that Noe could manage as she stood at the base of the rock and looked up at them.

"The Amberonks didn't work," said Radiah, her eyes almost flashing through tears. "Just like your plan didn't work. Just like Erica's plan didn't work. I'm sick of plans. We knew how to deal with the Smashed Man. We were dealing with the Smashed Man. We were fine."

"We weren't fine," said Crystal.

"Okay. We weren't fine, but we were surviving until the day we would be fine," said Radiah. "Now we've lost both Erica and . . ." A huge sobbed leaped from her chest and choked off her sentence.

"The Amberonks must work," said Noe.

"Because your gut told you they did?" said Radiah, shaking her head.

"What happened to Ruthy . . . that means the Smashed Man is still in the neighborhood. So Fern was right about him being trapped. That means the Amberonks work. And we know the Nonatuke works. You guys can't see the white house. The sigils work." She ignored the pestering voice in her head that wanted to bring up the two times the Elberex hadn't worked. "Did one of the Amberonks get rubbed off Ruthy's house?"

Crystal shook her head. "They were all there. Radiah and I checked."

"Where did they find her?"

"In her bed," said Radiah. She slumped on the top of the rock, as if that one outburst of anger was all she could manage. When Noe saw that, she almost starting crying again. She knew what Ruthy meant to Radiah. It would be like her losing Len. Noe turned her head to the side to hide her watery eyes, looking intently into Old Man Woods, at the green boughs, the gray rocks, the brown stream, the silver streaks of birch. Was the Smashed Man out there right now, hiding somewhere?

"What do we do?" asked Crystal. She was also looking away from the other girls, so it seemed like she was asking the forest.

"Something. We have to do something," said Noe, even though a big part of her felt as if she had lost the standing now to suggest that they do anything. "For our own safety. To get back at him for what he did to Ruthy. Because doing nothing now makes no sense." Her head dropped. She wasn't even sure if she was convincing herself.

"I agree."

Noe raised her head in surprise at what Radiah had said. "You do?"

"At this point, I don't care if the Smashed Man takes me in my sleep or jumps me on the way to the mailbox. It doesn't matter anymore. We might as well do something. Although what that something would be, I have no idea."

"We've learned a lot about the Smashed Man," said Noe.

"We have?" asked Crystal.

"We've learned he doesn't go after adults. Ruthy's dad is fine, right?"

"Or he can only go after one person a night. Or one a week or something like that. Like panthers," said Radiah. "Once they take down a full-grown deer, they don't need to eat for days. When they're full you could walk right in front of one and it wouldn't even twitch a whisker at you."

"That's possible," said Noe, picking a short, thick stick off the ground. "But we also know that he doesn't kill people. Not right out. Erica and Ruthy are in comas. Maybe he keeps them alive for other reasons." She held the stick in her fist like she was about to stab something with it. "Have you ever read *Dracula*?"

"I've seen a few movies," said Radiah. Crystal shook her head.

"In the book, Dracula has to feed off his victims three times before they become a vampire. If that's true in some way for the Smashed Man, that means both Erica and Ruthy—as long as they keep her at the hospital—are safe, since the Smashed Man is trapped here at Dread End."

"If those Amberonks even work," said Radiah.

"What good is all this guesswork?" asked Crystal.

"Every monster has rules, remember? Werewolves, vampires, mummies. They all have rules for what they can and cannot do. We know he had to be let out of the wall by a kid. We know he can only be active at night. We know adults can't see him. The Smashed Man has rules. And that means we just need to learn the most important rule about him: what stops him." Noe threw the stick at the ground, where it stuck in a patch of soft moss.

"But how do we do that? We don't have any information. Fern is gone and probably couldn't have helped us anyway. There's nothing we can do," said Crystal.

"All these rules only really mean that we don't know anything," said Radiah.

"Then what are we going to do?" asked Crystal.

"I think we should have a sleepover," said Noe.

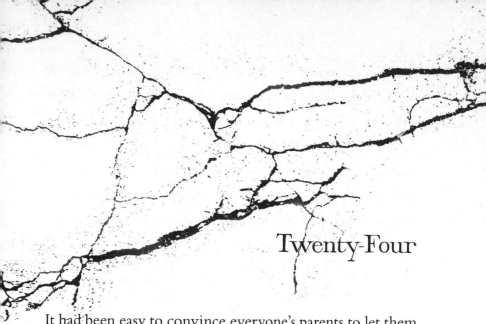

## Twenty-Four

It had been easy to convince everyone's parents to let them all sleep over at Radiah's that night. Because of Ruthy's condition, they could have asked for anything and gotten it. But the sleepover was what they wanted.

The shrinking group of Dread Enders had been hanging out in Radiah's attic since before dark. It was ten p.m. now, full dark, and Noe was standing at the window looking at her house, while Crystal and Radiah sat on the old rug on the floor playing games on their phones. It was strange to see her house from across the street. Noe was more used to the inside of the house than the outside. For instance, she had forgotten that they had a Pilgrim for a weather vane, the silhouette of which was now lost in the darkness. Along with her entire house, in fact. Her house was far enough back from the road that it seemed to disappear against the dark forest behind it. If it weren't for the light on the porch and the lights in the windows, it could have been as invisible as the white house.

One of those lights was from Len's room. She hated leaving Len behind, but she had made sure that the Amberonks were all in place before she crossed the street. Noe still believed in the Amberonks. She had to. What else did she have to believe in?

The girls had decided that the best thing for them to do would be to watch over the neighborhood. Radiah's attic room seemed the best place for that, since it was higher up and they could see a large section of the dead end from its window. They took turns, not sure what they were really looking for or hoping to see . . . or not see. Noe paid the closest attention to her house. She was really worried about Len.

She was also worried about what had happened to Ruthy. She couldn't understand how the Amberonks had failed at Ruthy's house. Noe had checked all the walls of Ruthy's house herself earlier that day, and Crystal was right. They were all still there, the big black R's dark and shimmery.

But the sleepover wasn't merely out of a sense of duty to the neighborhood. It was also for comfort. If the Smashed Man was going to come for them, he was going to have to face all of them. Even though none of them had put it in those words.

But there was one other thing she was worried about. The last time she had a sleepover at a friend's house, she had hurt that friend in her sleep. She had carefully explained to Radiah and Crystal about Abby and told them it was okay if they didn't want her over. "I can't help myself when it happens," Noe warned.

"We've slept above a monster all our lives," Radiah told her. "We're not afraid of you. We'll be fine." Crystal nodded her head. Noe had wanted to hug them both.

Noe was about to turn around and ask for one of the other Dread Enders to take a shift when she saw light down the street. Soon that light split into a pair of headlights, followed by the sound of an engine. She couldn't tell whose car it was in the dark, but if it was headed onto a dead end, it was either somebody who lived here or somebody who was turning around.

The car pulled up in front of Ruthy's house and a man got out. He left the door open, the headlights on, and the engine running as he followed the walkway to the front door of the house. It was Ruthy's dad.

"Mr. Larson's home," said Noe. Crystal and Radiah left their phones on the floor and clustered around Noe to see.

"Is Ruthy with him?" asked Crystal.

"He's alone."

"He's been at the hospital with Ruthy all day," said Radiah.

Mr. Larson walked to the house. The front overhang hid him once he got to the door, but a few seconds later, light spilled out onto the front lawn. He had opened the door.

"Bet you he doesn't shut it," said Radiah. "He forgets to a lot."

They all stared at the illuminated grass like they were waiting for an actor to enter a stage. Ten minutes later, Mr. Larson returned with a suitcase. He threw it in the back seat of the car and returned inside.

"It's going to be a long hospital stay," said Radiah.

"Like Erica," said Crystal.

"People must be able to see a connection, right? Two mysterious comas in two kids on the same street?" said Noe.

"Adults are blind," said Radiah. "Plus, who knows what they'd come up with as the answer? Definitely not a two-dimensional monster from outside the universe."

The light flowing onto the lawn went dark, and Mr. Larson came out of the house again, this time carrying a backpack and the stuffed penguin from Ruthy's room. Noe almost broke down when she saw that. She could feel Crystal and Radiah going through the same emotions on either side of her. He put the backpack and the penguin in the car. He started to get in and paused, then turned and headed back to the house. The porch lit up as he went inside.

Soon after a shadow flickered in the light, but the man who came out next was not Mr. Larson.

The three girls in the window froze, and Noe heard Crystal yelp.

The Smashed Man wobbled across the front lawn. Seeing him in an open space was strange. He walked like he was underwater, or like he was water, with ripples and waves running through his flat body. Under the right circumstances, the way he walked might have been hilarious.

But these weren't the right circumstances.

The Smashed Man stopped halfway across the lawn, wavering there like a plant in a windstorm.

"What's he doing?" whispered Radiah.

Before anybody could answer, the light on the porch turned off and they heard the front door shut. Mr. Larson came out carrying a grocery bag.

"Oh no," said Crystal.

"We've got to stop him!" said Radiah, sticking her fingers under the edge of the window to throw it open.

"Wait. I don't think Mr. Larson is in danger," said Noe.

Mr. Larson walked across the lawn, the grocery bag

held in front of him in both hands. It wasn't blocking his vision. He could see everything between him and the car. But he wasn't reacting to the terrifying creature on his front lawn. He walked past the Smashed Man, pushed the bag into the passenger seat of the car, and then got in and shut the door. Two minutes later, he was leaving Totter Court.

And the entire time, the Smashed Man stood there.

Noe kept waiting for him to turn his head, to look directly up at the girls. To let them know he knew exactly where they were and that he was coming for them.

Except he never did. When he finally moved, it was down the street the way Mr. Larson had gone. He soon disappeared in the darkness.

"Where's he going?" asked Radiah.

"To test the edges of his trap?" said Noe. That would mean he would make it as far as the Dread End sign. She looked over at Ruthy's witch house. The overhang hid the front door, so she couldn't see the Amberonk they had painted on it. She could see most of the side of the house, but the Amberonk and the house and the night were all overlapping darknesses that she couldn't parse. "Oh no," said Noe.

"What's the matter?" asked Crystal.

Noe walked away from the window to pace around the small cleared space in the attic. Crystal watched her, while Radiah kept an eye on the neighborhood, waiting for the Smashed Man to return. "We know that the Amberonks keep him inside the neighborhood. And that they should keep him out of our houses." She did another circuit around the room. "We've been in this attic since before dark but didn't see the Smashed Man enter Ruthy's house. That means he's probably been there since at least last night. It's also been dark for two hours now, and the Smashed Man only left Ruthy's house when Mr. Larson opened the door." Noe stopped by Radiah's desk and stared down at an eerily lifelike pencil drawing of the Smashed Man extruding out of a basement wall. "Wow. This is awesome, Radiah."

Radiah turned her head from the window and saw what Noe was talking about. "Thanks." She turned back to the window.

Noe continued to stare at the drawing. Radiah had captured perfectly the maniac grin, the wounds on his face, the rags embedded in his skin, the darkness of the basement around him, although she couldn't tell whose basement it was. And then something Radiah had said a few minutes before hit her. "We've made a big mistake," she said. She almost wasn't surprised. Everything she had tried since moving to this neighborhood had been a big mistake.

"What?" asked Crystal. Radiah might have echoed the

word, but Noe wasn't sure since she stayed glued to the window.

"Where's the Nonatuke on the white house painted?"

"On the front of the house," said Crystal.

"Right. But not on the front door, right?"

"What are you getting at?" asked Radiah, still staring through the window.

"I think that if the Nonatuke was painted on the front door of the white house, it would blink into existence every time Fern opened the front door."

"I don't get it," said Crystal. "Please just tell me."

Radiah turned from the window. "The Smashed Man only exited Ruthy's house just now because Mr. Larson opened the door. Opening the door broke the border because the Amberonk was on the door, not the wall. He probably left the door open at some point after dark last night, and the Smashed Man got in. And that means if anybody opens their front door at night, the Smashed Man can get in."

"Might be worse than that," said Noe. "Maybe he was in Ruthy's house the whole time. Maybe we trapped him inside when we painted the Amberonks on."

"Oh no," said Crystal.

"We have to fix this tonight," said Noe.

Radiah turned back to the window and nodded. "Here he comes."

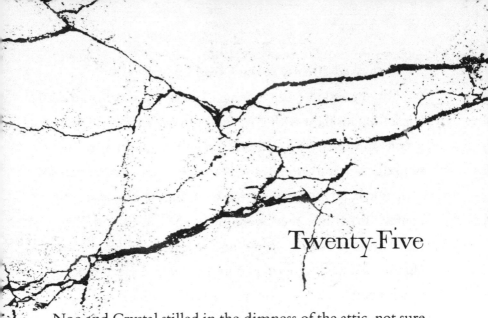

# Twenty-Five

Noe and Crystal stilled in the dimness of the attic, not sure which direction to run—away from the window or toward it. When they saw that Radiah hadn't flinched from her perch overlooking the neighborhood, they joined her, gingerly peering through the window as if they were afraid the Smashed Man would be inches away from the glass.

But he was still down the street, undulating up the middle of the dark pavement like he'd been copied from a different reality and pasted badly into this one. His head twisted slowly back and forth to take in the houses on either side of the street, but his face, what they could see of it in the dim streetlights, remained that same tortured mask. They watched him wobble closer until he was directly across from Radiah's house. He stopped, his flat head turning toward the house.

He looked directly at the Dread Enders.

His expression didn't change. His face was still stained black from his fight with Noe, making him look even more insane and terrifying. He stared at them. Crystal started whimpering and Noe wanted to dive beneath Radiah's bed, but Radiah returned his gaze like it was a staring contest. It felt like they were all trapped in that moment for hours, nothing changing, nothing moving, but eventually the Smashed Man turned his head and started walking toward Noe's house on the far side of the street.

That loosened Noe from the moment. "He's going to my house! To Len! We've got to get over there!"

Radiah put a hand on her arm and stopped her from diving headfirst down the attic stairs. "Look," she said.

The Smashed Man's turn toward the house was actually a turn toward the forest between Noe's house and the white house. He disappeared into the darkness of the trees. Noe imagined the sound he must have made, walking unsteadily through the dry leaves and underbrush, knowing that had she been in her own room, she would have heard it and dismissed it as a squirrel or a possum.

"You're right, Noe," said Radiah. "The Amberonks work. They keep him out of the houses. As long as nobody opens their front door."

"Just the front door? What about back doors?" asked Crystal.

"Those should be fine," said Noe. "We painted all the other Amberonks on actual walls on the other sides of the houses, right? It's just the front doors that we screwed up on."

"How are we going to fix them?" asked Radiah.

"We repaint them," said Noe. "Right now."

Radiah looked at her strangely, and Crystal seemed like she was about to crumple onto the rug.

"You guys don't have to go out there with me," said Noe. "We don't all need to do this. But I do. I need to make sure Len is okay. I need to make sure we don't end up like Ruthy and Erica." Noe sighed. "This is my fault. Ruthy shouldn't be in the hospital. The Smashed Man shouldn't be out there in the neighborhood."

"It's not your fault," said Crystal, almost too quietly.

"It is," said Noe.

"It . . . kind of . . . is," agreed Radiah.

"No! It's my fault!" shouted Crystal, her eyes brimming with tears. "I'm the reason the Smashed Man is out! I'm the reason Ruthy got hurt! I messed this whole thing up!"

Noe and Radiah looked at Crystal in confusion.

"Your plan," said Crystal. "I didn't do my part in your plan. I couldn't stand down there and face the Smashed Man. I tried. I went down there the first time. I saw him start coming out of the wall and I . . . ran back upstairs. I didn't go back down again after that." She sat down hard on the bed and continued to speak through her tears.

"But you texted us," said Noe.

"I stayed upstairs the whole time. He wasn't weak enough for you to attack with the darkwash because of that. It's my fault for being stupid and scared and now Ruthy's in the hospital and the Smashed Man is out there and somebody else will get hurt and you both will hate me." She started bawling.

"You just . . . lied?" shouted Noe. "I don't . . . I can't believe it."

"Is that why you've been acting so weird?" asked Radiah. Crystal let out a loud sob, and Radiah raised both of her hands in the air like she could magically calm Noe down and ease Crystal's crying simultaneously. "It's okay."

"No, it isn't," said Noe. "She put my life at risk. She put all our lives at risk. It's her fault Ruthy—"

"Don't you dare," said Radiah in a voice that was so calm it was almost threatening. She walked over to Crystal, who continued to cry, and put an arm around her. "Don't listen to her, Crystal. I totally understand. Noe doesn't know what it's like to live so many years in fear of that thing. She wasn't around when Erica got hurt."

Crystal looked up through her tears and said, "I was so scared. I couldn't help myself."

Noe immediately cooled. *I couldn't help myself.* Those were the same words she used herself when she thought about Abby and about her own sleepwalking. Noe went over and put her hand on Crystal's back. Her fingers overlapped with Radiah's as they did so, but neither of them pulled away.

"Radiah's right. It's okay. I'm sorry for getting angry," said Noe.

"But you're right to be," said Crystal.

"No, I'm not," said Noe. "There was never a guarantee that the plan would work in the first place. It might not have worked if we'd have pulled him out of the wall for eight straight days. It might never have worked. I was desperate. I needed to do something, and I didn't know what else to do."

Radiah looked at Noe. "But we know what to do right now. Tonight. We all do."

Noe nodded her head. "Now that he's off in the forest, I'm tempted to wait until morning. What are the chances someone opens their front door in the middle of the night?" Noe wasn't tempted at all, but she still wanted to give her friends a way out of what was about to happen.

Crystal wiped her eyes with her forearm and shook her head vigorously. "We have to do it tonight. What if Len sleepwalks and opens the door? What if my parents open the door and he slips inside my house and gets trapped there again? Or anybody's house? We shouldn't take any chances. Let's go to the white house, get the darkwash, and get this done."

"Wait here," said Radiah. "We're going to need a few things first." She walked down the stairs, hitting the dangling chain on the light bulb on her way. Before it had finished dancing, she was back in the attic with three plastic red buckets nested within each other. "We need to do this fast. We can't lug that giant tub of darkwash around in a wagon this time." She shoved the buckets at Crystal and then walked over to her dresser. She opened a drawer and pulled out a long, thin leather cord on which dangled a smooth rock with a hole through it. A witch rock.

"Is that Ruthy's?" asked Crystal.

"No. It's Erica's."

"Erica never had a witch rock."

"I found one for her. It was the day before . . . the Smashed Man got her. I never got to give it to her." Radiah approached Noe. "You should wear this. It may not help against the Smashed Man, but it means you're one of us. A Dread Ender." Noe lifted up her hair and let Radiah tie the leather in a knot behind her neck. The rock felt solid against her chest. She tested the weight of it in her hand for a second and then let it drop back. It felt good.

They headed down the attic stairs and through the hallway, past Radiah's parents' bedroom. They could hear the box fan whirring away, the kind of noise that would wake most people up instead of putting them to sleep like the Harrises. Noe and Radiah and Crystal walked downstairs to the front door, where they clustered around the side windows, trying to see if the Smashed Man was wobbling his way back from the forest. The street was empty and dark.

"I think we should run," said Noe. She reached into her pocket and pulled out the small stainless-steel key to the white house like it was a weapon.

Radiah opened the door a crack. "Remember, we can't see this place. You have to lead us in."

Noe nodded. "Stay close to me, and when we get to the porch, Radiah, you grab my hand, and Crystal, you grab hers. Everybody ready?" Radiah nodded, while Crystal held the nested buckets tighter. Noe threw one more look into the bulb of the dead end to make sure it was empty, half hoping it wasn't so that they would have to stay inside and hide from the Smashed Man. It was empty. "Let's go!"

Noe was off, taking a direct line between Radiah's house and the white house and hoping Crystal and Radiah were behind her. By the sound of shoe rubber on asphalt, the two were sticking extremely close. They were halfway to the white house when Crystal screamed, "There he is!"

Noe looked over at the edge of the forest where they had last seen the monster. He was coming at them, and he was coming fast. His rippling, physics-defying gait had sped into a terrifying sprint. Like he was being fast-forwarded, like he was flowing through the air and the night instead of moving across the ground. His arms were waving rapidly in front of him. His face was a darkwash-stained leer.

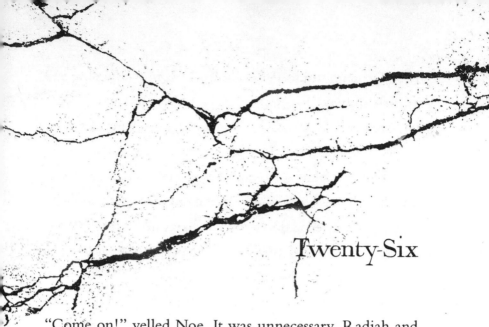

# Twenty-Six

"Come on!" yelled Noe. It was unnecessary. Radiah and Crystal passed her like she was walking, even though the white house was invisible to them. She could see that both were focused on the area directly in front of them, neither looking over at the Smashed Man. She followed their lead, focusing where they couldn't—on the Amberonk painted on the front door of the white house. Crystal and Radiah slowed slightly when they made it to the edge of the asphalt to let Noe surge ahead, the key in one hand and her other extended to Radiah. She held Radiah's hand tight as Radiah grabbed Crystal's hand.

Noe jumped up the stairs with the other girls in tow and shoved the key in the lock, hoping the door wasn't dead-bolted. She twisted the knob and slammed through with her shoulder. It gave, and she pulled Radiah and Crystal behind her.

Noe stumbled to Fern's camp chair, took a breath, and turned around.

She saw the Smashed Man running up the front lawn.

Nobody had shut the door.

Radiah apparently realized it at the same time. "Shut the door!" she screamed to Crystal, who was the closest to it. Crystal turned and froze, the buckets held limply in one hand as she stared at the Smashed Man rushing at her like she was in her basement alone with him.

Noe laughed so hard she almost collapsed the camp chair as she leaned on it.

Radiah ran at the door and slammed it shut, locking both the doorknob and dead bolt, and then sprinted across the room to where Noe was. "Why are you laughing?"

Noe kept laughing as she waded through the mess on the floor of the living room to the window with the broken glass that faced behind the house, cupping her hand around her eyes to look through into the darkness. "Look." She pointed at something outside.

After stealing a quick glance at the locked door, Radiah walked over to the window, followed by Crystal.

"He's behind the house!" said Radiah. The Smashed Man was twenty feet away, spinning around slowly, his horrible face twisting back and forth on his neck. The way his body wavered, he looked like a glitch in the forest.

"What's he doing?" asked Crystal.

"He can't see the house," said Noe. "I could tell by the angle he was running on the front lawn. It was . . . off. Like when Radiah tried to prove this house didn't exist . . . and now he's exactly where Radiah ended up."

"He can't see the house," said Radiah.

"He can't see the house!" yelled Crystal, grabbing Radiah and hugging her. Radiah hugged her back just as hard. "Can we all move in here until we become adults?" Crystal laughed and let Radiah go. After a stutter of her arms, Crystal hugged Noe too.

"Let's get that darkwash," said Noe.

It took them a little bit of effort to pour the giant white bucket of darkwash into the smaller red buckets that Radiah had found for them. By the time they were finished, they had three full buckets and a carpet stained with large blobs of the stuff. It didn't make the room seem any messier.

Each girl took a paintbrush, leaving the fourth one, Ruthy's, lying on the carpet beside the spilled darkwash.

"Which house first?" asked Crystal.

"This one, I guess?" said Noe. "I mean, he can't see it, but that doesn't mean he might not find his way in. You guys are in here and you can't see it."

"It would be the easiest house to do," said Crystal.

239

"Is he still out there?" asked Radiah, looking over at the window.

Noe peeked out but saw only darkness and hints of trees. "No. Let me check out front." She walked over to the front door, a red bucket of darkwash in one hand and a paintbrush in the other. She looked through the peephole. Nothing out there. "All right." She twisted the locks on the dead bolt and the doorknob, and then flung the door open wide.

Nothing moved on the street.

"He can't see us or hear us as long as we're in here," said Noe, although whether that was to reassure her friends or herself, she didn't know. She stuck the brush in the bucket of darkwash and then leaned out and quickly painted an Amberonk on the wall beside the door before diving back in. "That easy," she said, although she wondered briefly if two Amberonks canceled each other out, like two negative numbers in math. And then she thought about how weird it was to have XRR painted on the front of the house, like a vandal's initials.

They all looked through the open door at the darkness of Dread End, pockets of which were alleviated by the light from the streetlamps lining the road. Most of the porches were alive with light, like little islands in the night. Nobody said anything. The next step would be an extremely difficult one.

"I don't think I can run out there again," said Noe.

"Me either," said Radiah.

"We're going to have to, though, right?" said Crystal.

Neither Radiah nor Noe answered. They all gazed out at Dread End.

Finally Radiah spoke. "I need a pencil and paper."

The items were easy to find, and soon the three girls were on the floor crowded around a large yellow pad. Radiah had sketched out Dread End with little rectangles for the houses. She drew lines between the houses and numbered them as she explained exactly how they would get new Amberonks on all the houses without being exposed outside for too long.

"Hold on. Here's an idea. Maybe we only have to do your house and my house," said Noe to Radiah. "We just saw Mr. Larson walk right past the Smashed Man. The adults are fine. And your house and my house are the only ones with kids in it tonight. Then tomorrow we fix the rest of the houses, just in case."

"Are we sure?" asked Radiah, still gazing out into the neighborhood, waiting for the Smashed Man to wobble his way across the road.

"Sure about what?" asked Noe.

"Sure that there are no other kids on this block tonight. Are we sure nobody's nieces or nephews or grandchildren are visiting? Do we know that for sure?"

"No. We have to paint Amberonks on all the houses tonight," said Crystal.

"If we'd only done it right the first time," said Noe.

"We didn't know," said Radiah, staring down at the plan she had sketched.

"I should have tried harder to meditate. To see if there was an answer there." Noe found her own statement silly. She didn't even understand what she'd been shown during her first meditation.

Radiah half smiled. "It doesn't matter. We're about to fix it. Everybody got the plan?"

Noe nodded. So did Crystal, as she stared into the dimness of the neighborhood. "Where is he?"

"He probably gave up after we disappeared. Maybe he's testing the other side of the trap, somewhere near Rune Rock," said Noe.

"That would mean he's deep in Old Man Woods. That'd be perfect for us," said Radiah.

"Or he could be out there on the edge of the woods, waiting for us to come out," said Crystal.

The three girls huddled in the doorway, looking for any unearthly movement. The only motion they saw were dots of bugs swarming around the streetlights and a single bat flapping around and feasting on the dots. Noe got her home key ready.

"Go," whispered Radiah.

Noe ran to her house. It took seconds to get there, seconds to paint an Amberonk on the wall—a slash of a vertical line, a hump, and a tail—and seconds to open her front door and jump inside. She looked across the street and saw that Crystal and Radiah were safe in Radiah's doorway, a fresh black R on the wall beside them.

That's all it took. Seconds. They could do this.

Crystal held up her hand, three fingers in the air above her and Radiah's heads. Noe focused on it. Crystal lowered a finger to start the countdown. The second she was down to her fist, Noe burst from her house, leaving her front door wide open. She could do that now that the Amberonk was painted on the front wall instead of the door, and she headed to the gray house beside hers, bucket of darkwash in hand. Radiah did the same but headed to Ruthy's. Ten seconds to get there. Five seconds to grab the brush out of the bucket and paint the Amberonk. Ten seconds to run back to the welcoming open door of her own house. Only half a minute. She looked across the street and saw Radiah back with Crystal.

The next set of houses would take twice as long, meaning they would be exposed for twice as long. But twice as long was only a minute. She looked across the street. Radiah was counting down this time, with Crystal poised with bucket and brush to take the next run.

When Radiah clenched her fist, Noe and Crystal took off. Past the houses on which they had just painted Amberonks to the next houses on the block. Quickly up the steps. Quickly painting the Amberonk, quickly back to their open doorways.

Seven houses done. Six left. But the rest were so far away.

Fortunately, Crystal's home was one of the remaining houses.

This next part of Radiah's plan was the hardest. The three would take off together. Radiah would paint Amberonks on the three remaining houses on her side of the street. Noe would do the same on hers, skipping Crystal's house. Crystal would run straight to her house, paint an Amberonk on it, and then open the door so Noe and Radiah could dash inside when they were done. All three would be running through the neighborhood fully exposed, hoping the Smashed Man was still somewhere out by Rune Rock.

Radiah's fingers, Radiah's fist, and all three girls ran into the night, buckets and brushes ready like shields and swords.

Noe hit the next house that needed an Amberonk on her side of the street, which turned out to be Mrs.

Washington's house. As soon as she jumped onto the porch, she realized this house didn't need a new Amberonk. Its previous sigil was at the corner of the facade because that was where Radiah had painted it while the rest of them were distracting Mrs. Washington out front. The house was safe. Noe cringed at the time she'd wasted, leaped down the steps, and dashed across the lawn as fast as she could. She didn't see Crystal until too late.

Crystal was crossing Mrs. Washington's lawn, trying to get to her own house next door. The two girls twisted desperately away from each other at the last second, their plastic buckets hitting each other and clacking loudly in the night. Noe felt her bucket pulled from her hand as the handles got tangled. It flew across the lawn and landed with a soft thump on its side in the grass.

Crystal spun around in surprise and horror while Noe dived for her bucket. She righted it with about a quarter of the liquid left inside. The rest formed a pool on Mrs. Washington's lawn that looked like it was reflecting the night sky above, even though it was full of its own stars.

Noe looked up and saw Radiah across the street, almost done with the three houses she had to do, while she and Crystal hadn't even done one. She looked up to make sure Crystal was opening the door to her house . . . and saw the Smashed Man running hard down the middle of the street, his body flapping like he was running against a strong wind and his purple eyes the brightest points in the entire neighborhood. Crystal screamed.

"Get in your house!" yelled Noe, jumping up and grabbing the bucket and brush. Crystal turned around and ran, Noe following behind her.

Crystal ran to her front door and jiggled the key in the lock, while Noe stood behind her, aching with the need to get behind that door with the Amberonk on it. She turned and saw that the Smashed Man was almost to the edge of the lawn.

And she knew Crystal wouldn't get the door open in time.

Noe jumped down the steps and ran at the Smashed Man.

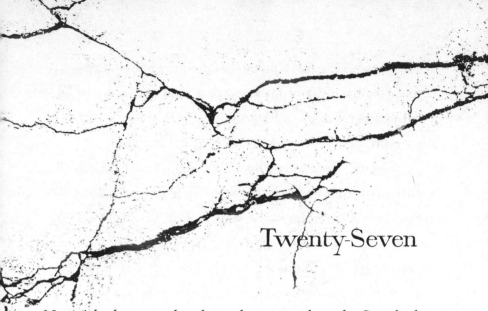

# Twenty-Seven

Noe picked up speed and got close enough to the Smashed Man that he reached his flat arms out for her, like when he would come out of the basement wall, but at the last second, she pivoted and ran toward the open end of the street.

She looked over her shoulder and saw that the Smashed Man was only a few arm's lengths behind her. The relief she felt that he wasn't going after Crystal, that Crystal would have time to get safely into her house, lasted only half a step before turning into horror. She wanted to drop right there in the middle of the street and curl into a ball and let the Smashed Man get her. Like Len would do when Noe chased her around the house howling like a werewolf. But then Noe had a better idea.

Her lungs ached and her legs wobbled and she was sweating in the summer night, but she finally saw what she was looking for: a metal diamond on a post. It rose five feet into the air, and she knew that the front was a beautiful yellow with black letters and a glittery Amberonk that marked the edge of the Smashed Man's cage.

She sped past the Dread End sign and stopped. She turned around and saw that so had the Smashed Man. He was only five feet away from her, but he wasn't lunging after her. His arms weren't even raised. He stood there wavering like a flame and staring like a madman, his purple eyes trained on her as if he was waiting for her to say something.

She had nothing to say. It was all she could do to keep from screaming.

The Smashed Man stared at Noe as he bobbed up and down on his wobbly legs. They were directly under a streetlamp, and she could see that the skin and bare muscle and bone of his face were still stained black from their encounter in her basement.

The adrenaline that fueled her across the border fled her just as fast, and she doubled over, gulping in deep breaths and trying not to panic from being mere feet away from the monster.

He was terrifying. Even across an uncrossable border. She felt like she was going to throw up. She didn't know what type of scared this was. Just that she needed to sit down. To lie down. To curl into a ball and whimper. She wanted to run away from the neighborhood. To run all the way across town. To run back to her old house. To run back in time to before she ever lived here.

She felt the hard rectangle of her phone in her pocket. She couldn't call her parents. Couldn't scream into the night for help. Bringing adults here to drag her back across the border would be as good as throwing herself to the Smashed Man.

She put the bucket of darkwash on the ground and paced back and forth, hoping it would break the Smashed Man's silent stare. It didn't. His head followed her movements with the patience of a monster that had been stuck in a basement crack for decades, starting his escape over and over again until he finally made it out. Until Noe finally helped him make it out.

She was having trouble focusing. Her clothes were heavy and sticky with sweat and the bugs seemed to be getting louder and the Smashed Man wouldn't stop looking at her and her entire world was ten feet of asphalt and grass and she was sharing that world with a monster.

Her exhaustion gave her the only idea it could.

She was going to lie down in the grass and go to sleep.

It was a brilliant plan.

Really, all she had to do was wait for dawn, for the sun

to chase the Smashed Man back into a crevice somewhere. She almost smiled. That crevice would have to be somewhere out in the woods. All the houses on Totter Court were protected now, thanks to the Dread Enders.

She pulled her phone out of her pocket and tapped at the glass until she got the answer she needed. Sunrise was at five twenty-three a.m. Only about five hours away. She tapped again at the phone screen, this time writing a message to Radiah and Crystal, wherever they were: **I'm OK. Outside Totter. SM can't get me but won't let me come back. I'll sleep here till day. Parents will think I sleepwalked.** She finished it with a sleepy face emoji.

She didn't hit send. The last word in her message chilled her.

Sleepwalking was the perfect alibi for being outside in the neighborhood all night, but what if it ended up being true? What if she fell asleep right there, and then stood up and walked into the arms of the Smashed Man?

The Smashed Man continued to stare at her as if that was exactly what he was waiting for.

She would have to stay up all night. That was the only way to guarantee her safety. But even as she thought that, she realized it would be impossible. She was too tired. She'd have to move, now.

She made the decision in a second. She retrieved the

bucket of darkwash, then walked right up to the Smashed Man until he was inches away, barely the width of the border separating them. She could see the texture in his glowing purple irises; the slit of darkness between his teeth; the stringy, oily blackness of his hair; the moistness of the exposed muscle and bone in his cheeks and forehead and on his arms and legs.

She threw the bucket of black goo at his face.

It hit him full-on, a torrent of thick blackness obscuring his features. He staggered back, clawing and tearing at his face like she had thrown burning tar on it.

She threw down the bucket and ran past him.

She could see that Crystal's front door wasn't open, so she aimed for Radiah's, deeper within the dead end. However, as she passed the first house on the block, she realized that not all the houses on Totter Court were protected after all. She'd missed painting a new Amberonk on the last one on this side of the street.

She snuck a glance over her shoulder and saw the Smashed Man capering about near the Dread End sign, swiping at his face and jiggling around like a puppet with a bad puppeteer.

She altered her course and swung by the front porch of the house. She had used all the darkwash on the Smashed Man, but she still had a brush in her hand covered in it.

She painted the fastest Amberonk of the night on the wall beside the door with their previous Amberonk on it, barely pausing to change her trajectory to continue to Radiah's house. She didn't turn around to see if the Smashed Man was chasing her, because it didn't matter if he was or not. It only mattered that she ran as fast as she could.

For a second, she wondered if she should run to her house instead, since she had the key. But an open door and two girls standing underneath a porch light told her that she was running exactly where she needed to run.

Radiah and Crystal jumped up and down when they saw her, their arms waving in come-here-fast gestures, as if that would help Noe run faster. It did.

She sprinted across Radiah's lawn, and the two girls moved inside the door. Noe tumbled in after them, with Crystal and Radiah grabbing her to absorb the force so she didn't smack facefirst into a wall.

Nobody shut the front door right away. There was no need to. The Amberonks were all on solid, unmoving walls now, protecting the entire house.

The Smashed Man was nowhere to be seen.

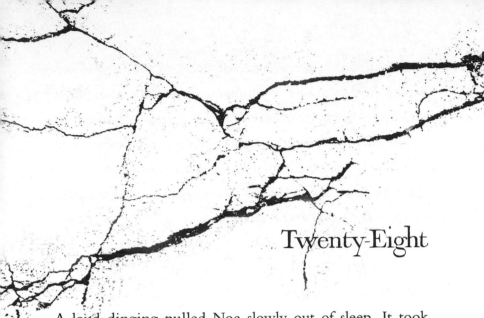

## Twenty-Eight

A loud dinging pulled Noe slowly out of sleep. It took her a long time to piece together where she was. She saw dirty rafters. Cobwebs. Cardboard boxes scribbled on with black marker. Furniture legs. She was lying on an old rug on the floor. For a moment she thought that she had been sleepwalking, but the pillow her head rested on and the blankets she was wrapped in went against that idea. Then she realized she was in an attic. Radiah's attic. She heard the dinging noise again and looked over at the white plastic box on the wall that was the intercom. She saw Radiah and Crystal slowly moving into wakefulness on Radiah's bed.

They looked fine, if bleary. She hadn't attacked them in her sleep.

"What does your mom want so early in the . . ." Crystal checked her phone. "Afternoon."

"That was some professional sleeping," said Noe, her jaw cracking through an immense yawn that communicated that her body wouldn't mind going back to work for another shift. The daylight leaking through the dirty window fought the dimness of the attic, catching clouds of glowing dust motes. Noe thought it was the most beautiful thing in the world at the moment.

The girls wandered downstairs, still in the same clothes from the previous night, to find a nice little summer feast laid out on the kitchen table. There were hot dogs and corn bread and cantaloupe slices and strawberries and a pitcher of the brightest yellow lemonade that Noe had ever seen. Noe felt like she hadn't eaten in a week.

Radiah's mother was flitting around the kitchen like she was an engineer in the engine room of a giant ship. "Good morning, sleepyheads," she greeted them. "I figured since you all missed breakfast, you might like a nice lunch."

"Thanks," all three said, more or less at the same time, as they dropped into the hard kitchen chairs around the table.

Radiah's mother placed deviled eggs in front of them and sat down in a chair. "So what adventures were you all up to last night?"

"Nothing much," said Radiah, grabbing two of the

deviled eggs and dropping them on her plate. "Played games."

"We did a little bit of painting," said Crystal, taking a bite out of a cantaloupe slice and not making eye contact with anyone.

"Hope you didn't make too much of a mess. But then again, it's the attic, so I guess it doesn't matter," sighed Mrs. Harris. "So, Miss Christmas, are your parents getting ready for the summer bonfire? It's next month, you know."

"I think so," Noe answered, pulling the green hair off a strawberry. "I guess I don't know what they have to do to get ready, though."

"Well, nothing really," said Mrs. Harris. "Other than gather all the stuff they want to burn from your yard. Everyone else will cart theirs over in wheelbarrows. Except Mr. Hanson. He always hooks up a wagon behind his riding lawn mower and drives it over. He loves driving that thing. And we all bring something to eat. A big potluck. I'm thinking I'll bring potato salad." Mrs. Harris tapped at her empty plate with a fork. "It won't be the same without Erica's family, but it'll still be fun. It's always fun. Goes late into the night. You'll have a good time. Isn't that right, girls?"

Neither Crystal nor Radiah answered, and all three girls looked like they were buffering, they were so still.

Noe was the first to say anything. "Late into the night?"

"Oh, sure. Everybody likes to stay up for it. We roast marshmallows and make s'mores. You know, like summer camp."

They continued to eat, although with much less enthusiasm and with Mrs. Harris doing most of the talking. Eventually they all finished and helped Mrs. Harris load the dishwasher.

"Everybody's going to be out of their houses at night," said Radiah once they were back in the attic. "I can't believe I didn't think of that."

"We never had a reason to be scared during the bonfires before," said Crystal. "The Smashed Man was always stuck in our basements."

"At least the adults are all safe," said Noe.

"We think," said Crystal. "Who knows why the Smashed Man ignored Ruthy's dad?"

"Yeah," said Noe. "But let's hope it's true. Because we'll have our hands full worrying about the three of us and Len."

"Can't we make another border around your yard?" asked Crystal.

Noe thought about it. "Maybe, but it seems complicated. With a house, we just protect each wall. Do we paint Amberonks on all the trees at the edge of my yard?

That's a lot of trees. And what about the spaces between them? And what about the parts that don't have trees, like most of the front lawn?"

"The Neighbors figured out how to do it," said Radiah.

"But Fern said that the Amberonks around the neighborhood are layered and interconnected. I don't know. I'd rather figure out how to keep us and Len inside my house while everybody else bonfires it up." Noe headed for the stairs. "I'm going home. I need a shower." Although what she really needed was not to have to worry about the Smashed Man ever again.

She left Radiah's house, throwing Mrs. Harris a quick "Thanks for breakfast!" as she passed her in the living room. Mrs. Harris was lying on the couch with a paperback book in one hand and her phone in the other. Noe walked out the door and across the asphalt, staring at the pair of Amberonks on the front of her house, one on the door and the other beside it on the wall. If they really were Egyptian Eyes of Horus, her house was staring at her right now, and it was thinking how bad she was at making plans that worked.

# Twenty-Nine

"I'll get it!" yelled Noe from her room. She was pretty sure that it was Radiah or Crystal knocking on her front door. For the past month, they had been desperately trying to figure out what to do about the summer bonfire. It was only a couple of days away now, and they didn't have a plan for staying inside their houses. They had thought about all of them faking sick, but that would leave Len on her own. Worse, the bonfire night was only part of a larger problem.

The Amberonks on the houses seemed to be working, but it was a short-term solution. They didn't have to worry about somebody opening a door at night anymore, but it was only a matter of time before a kid was caught outside after sunset, especially with fall and winter approaching. Sunset at its earliest during those seasons would be some-time between four and five o'clock, only an hour after school was let out. And that didn't even count the danger of Noe or Len sleepwalking outside.

Noe had been extra careful about that last issue, making sure the baby gate was always locked and tied with her robe sash every night. Tying herself to the bed. And sometimes even getting Len to sleep in her room. It had worked so far, but it also wasn't a permanent solution.

The only permanent solution was to get rid of the Smashed Man.

The Dread Enders would stare out their windows at night and see the Smashed Man wobbling furiously around the neighborhood, in and out of the forest, behind one house and in front of another, trying to find a victim or any way into a house or out of Totter Court. It was almost worse than when he was in their basements.

Ruthy was still at the hospital with no change in her condition. The big discussion among the adults in the neighborhood was whether Mr. Larson would try to find a specialist, like Erica's family had. Except that Erica was still in a coma, so it didn't seem worthwhile to sell his house and move to a faraway state yet. The girls had visited Ruthy twice so far. It was devastating to see her unconscious in a hospital bed.

Noe had even finally tried meditating to see if she could get any answers that way. She had been too embarrassed to try at home, but she had gone to the white house a few times and tried it. She hadn't been able to get it to work by herself, though, even with the metronome, and that depressed her. Fern had made it sound like all the answers she needed were just a meditation session away, but it hadn't turned out to be like that at all. The first time hadn't even done much other than chase Fern away.

Noe descended the stairs, half expecting her mother to beat her to the door and not at all expecting the person on the other side of the door when Noe opened it.

"Hello, young lady," Fern said, looking down at her like she didn't know who Noe was. "Is your mother or father at home?" She was holding a brochure in her hand.

"I'm her mother," said Mom. Noe hadn't seen Mom standing in the other room.

"Hello, ma'am. My name is Fern, and I'm handing out brochures for my new restaurant downtown." She handed the brochure to Mom.

Noe's mother looked it over and nodded her head. "I like Mexican food."

"Great! There's a coupon in there for twenty percent off. Please come on down. Kids eat half off on Sundays." She nodded down at Noe like Noe was six years old.

"Sure, we'll check it out," said Mom.

"Great! Have a good day, ma'am and ma'am," She bowed her head and left, the crutch clacking beside her.

"That was strange," said Mom after she'd closed the door.

"Why?" asked Noe.

"There's a mailing sticker on the back of this brochure with our address. Why would she hand-deliver that? Should have been in the mailbox with all the other junk mail." Her mom dropped the brochure on a side table. "What are you up to today?"

"Nothing much, but I think I left my phone at Radiah's house," said Noe. "I'll be right back."

"Okay, but your dad needs some help clearing brush at the edge of the yard for the bonfire, and I think somebody is bringing over tables. He might need help setting those up too."

Noe exited the house and started around the bulb of the driveway like she was taking her time to Radiah's house, in case Mom was watching out of the window. She even kicked a few stones on the way for good measure. Once she got to the white house, though, she saw the door standing open, so she disappeared inside immediately.

"Looks like this neighborhood has been vandalized." Fern was sitting in her camp chair with her elephant teacup in hand. On the cardboard box in front of her sat the matching tray and teapot and, Noe saw gratefully, another cup.

Noe poured herself some chai and settled back into the couch. "We were protecting it from the Smashed Man."

"You were acting foolish again." Fern sipped her tea. "Did it work?"

Noe told her the story, finishing up with the looming bonfire. "Can we use the Amberonks on the backyard?"

"No, that's silly. Houses only have four planes of protection, but for an open yard edged by a forest like yours, we're talking countless planes of protection. The Neighbors would all have to work on it for months to figure out that math. Best you and the others just stay inside during the bonfire." It was the same conclusion that the Dread Enders had come to already, so it wasn't too much of a disappointment for Noe.

Fern leaned closer, the red lenses of her glasses reflecting Noe's teacup. "I'd like to say that I'm impressed that you've faced down the Smashed Man twice now." She took a sip of tea, not looking at all impressed. "But it feels like you keep making your situation worse, and therefore my situation worse. Still, you might be interested in this." She plucked a flat wooden box about the width of the tea tray from the floor. It was polished to a deep brown and carved with intertwining palm trees and shorebirds. She handed it to Noe.

Noe opened the lid. Nestled on a cushion of shiny cream-colored silk were two rows of what looked like enamel pins. There were six of them, all iridescent purple, each flat and about four inches long, and not made of any material that Noe recognized. But she recognized the shapes.

They were sigils. An Amberonk, a Nonatuke, three whose names she didn't remember, if she had ever known them, and an Elberex.

"You froze the snake!"

"Not exactly," Fern said. "But it is solidified darkwash."

"What? How? Why? When?" Noe didn't know what question to ask, so she asked them all.

"Your cells, is the answer to most of those questions. That Erica girl's diary is the answer to the rest. Do you understand states of matter? Liquid, gas, solid, plasma? Do they teach that in New England schools?"

"Sure," said Noe, getting the word out of the way so that she could say the words that she really wanted to say. "Can I hold one?" When Fern shrugged, Noe went right for the Elberex.

"We had never considered the darkwash as having states before," said Fern. "In fact, all our experiments had us leaning toward it being a nonmaterial substance."

"But it's purple. How did you . . ." and then she remembered the end of her meditation session. "Heat," she finished.

"Yes, like in your meditation. But that wouldn't have been enough to give me the idea if I hadn't seen that girl's diary. I figured the darkwash must have congealed from all the weeks it was exposed to the heat of the dryer."

"So the heat turns it purple, too?" Like the black liquid darkwash, the solid sigils looked like they were full of twinkling stars, except against bright purple instead of black.

"It took an extreme level of heat to make those, and a lot of experimentation by some of the Neighbors to find the right method, but once we did . . ." Fern twirled a hand in the direction of the box.

"What are you going to do with these?" Noe asked.

Fern shrugged again and sipped her tea. "I don't know. We'll keep experimenting. Keep sorting through our subatomic particles, looking for answers." Fern placed her elephant teacup back on the tray. "Or we could sort through yours. Have you tried meditating since I've been gone?"

Noe nodded her head slightly.

"Did it work?"

She shook her head just as slightly.

"I want you to try again."

This time Noe shrugged. She had been hoping Fern would say that, because the only time she had been able to achieve a meditative state was with Fern. And if Fern could get it to work again, then maybe Noe could discover some answers. Any answers. She was desperate. Still, it didn't seem right to show Fern her eagerness, especially since Fern was treating her like a lab rat. Noe walked casually over to the corner while Fern got the metronome.

Noe settled down on the carpet. She still held the Elberex tightly in her hand. A few moments later, she heard the ticking start behind her. She relaxed into it and started her om chanting.

Entering the meditation was as difficult as it had been the first time, maybe even more so. She almost gave up multiple times, but the sight of Fern sitting in the camp chair staring at her like she expected her to fail made her keep trying.

Eventually, at some point, she wasn't sitting cross-legged in the corner of an invisible house on a residential street in Osshua with a woman who spoke in a Southern accent who Mom thought ran a Mexican restaurant. She was floating in blackness. That extremely familiar blackness. And as usual, she wasn't alone. But this time her companion wasn't the eyeless purple snake. It was the second phase of the creature. The solid darkwash Elberex, purple and glowing against the void.

The shimmering Elberex was floating away from her, pulling her behind it. The void seemed to close around her, like she was in a dark tunnel. Soon the darkness of the tunnel was ribbed with rings of bright white light, which she flew through, the ribs flashing past faster and faster as she picked up more speed.

And then she saw faces in the tunnel. Or rather on the

outside of the tunnel. White ovals in the blackness with empty black eyes and mouths, like featureless masks. But they weren't lifeless. She could feel their gazes as the faces popped in and out of existence.

The Elberex slowed. Stopped. Hovered. She did the same. The tunnel had disappeared, and they were once more in an inky void. The Elberex moved again, but not in a direction. It started moving around itself like the purple loops were a conveyor belt, speeding up until it seemed like it was about to fly apart. Noe started panicking, but she wasn't sure why.

The Elberex stopped.

A purple eye opened in each loop.

Noe threw her arms across her face in shock.

She found herself back in the corner of a ticking room on Dread End. It felt exactly like coming out of a sleep-walking episode. She grabbed at the pieces of reality and nightmare around her and tried to assemble them with numb fingers, wondering which pieces were real and which weren't, using them to pull herself back to herself.

The ticking behind her stopped. "What did you see?" asked Fern.

Noe moved the Elberex to her other hand and looked at the impression it had left on her skin from holding the object so tightly. "Weird stuff." As best she could, she described the tunnel and the faces and what happened to the Elberex. "Do you know what that all means?"

"Zero clue, girl. But cell knowledge is always gibberish to us at first. We're like two-year-olds trying to read an advanced physics textbook." But Fern sounded disappointed, and Noe felt like it was her fault.

Stepping back into the neighborhood from the invisible house was like coming back to all her problems—the Smashed Man, the summer bonfire, sleepwalking, protecting her little sister. But now she had strange images of tunnels and white-mask faces and solid darkwash. She looked down in her hand and realized she had kept the purple Elberex.

As she stared down at it, almost walking into one of the trees in her front yard in the process, something began to tickle in her mind. Something important. She wouldn't completely figure it out until later that night, in her bed, after she'd checked on the baby gate and Len.

Noe opened Erica's diary, flipping through the pages here and there and mostly looking at the sketches. She stopped at a large image of the Smashed Man's face. One with the Elberex on its forehead.

Maybe the vision had told her how to get rid of the Smashed Man. And maybe Erica's plan hadn't been too far off after all.

# Thirty

The day of the summer bonfire seemed far too hot to light a match, much less a giant fire. But that didn't seem to slow anybody in the neighborhood. Leading up to the fire, Noe watched people clean their lawns and cart brush over to her backyard. Some neighbors even hired professional tree cutters to take down dangerous limbs and trees. The tree cutters had giant cranes that soared up into the sky and were accompanied by men with loud, terrifying chain saws. The whole neighborhood seemed to be going through one of Mom's spring cleanings, except that she never burned unwanted toys and clothes at the end.

The bonfire started at six thirty, and it would be fully dark about two hours later. That was the scary time. The Dread Enders had a plan, but it was a loose one, with far too many places for it to go completely wrong.

Noe had been surprised that Crystal and Radiah had

gone along with her latest idea so willingly, after how many times she had messed up, but they did. Maybe a month trapped in their houses watching the monster roam the street was enough. Maybe they were just ready to be done with the Smashed Man for good, either way. Maybe they trusted her.

She looked out her window and saw Radiah and Crystal passing her mailbox. Just as Noe had suspected he would, Dad had eventually replaced the boring black mailbox with a more fanciful one. He had chosen a box shaped like a covered bridge. Radiah was carrying a bowl covered in cling wrap, and Crystal held a tray covered in aluminum foil. Noe grabbed a paintbrush off her dresser, stuck it in her back pocket, and raced down to meet them. As they walked up to her, her brain flashed a quick image of Radiah, Crystal, and Ruthy looming at the edge of her front yard when she had first moved in.

"Everything ready?" asked Radiah.

"Yup," Noe answered. "Food goes on the table in the backyard, the bonfire is prepped, and we start the party promptly at six thirty."

Radiah narrowed her eyes at her.

Noe lowered her voice. "There's a bucket of dark-wash hidden in the kitchen cabinet by the back door and another by the steps outside it. I have the Elberex here," She grabbed the leather cord that had been around her neck since Radiah had given her the witch stone and pulled it out of her T-shirt. Instead of the witch stone, the shimmery purple Elberex had been strung on it through its two loops. The other girls instinctively grabbed their witch stones. "Does everybody have their paintbrushes?"

Crystal and Radiah both turned slightly to show wooden handles sticking out of their back pockets.

"Where's Len?" asked Radiah.

"Here I am!" sang Len, suddenly behind Noe as if she had popped out of a gopher hole. She held a stuffed kiwi bird above her head with both hands. "Can I jump on your back?" she asked her big sister.

"No, I'm busy. Go help Dad . . . do something," said Noe.

"Come on!" said Len.

"You can jump on my back," said Crystal, handing her tray to Noe. Len beamed at her, and Crystal squatted down to let her climb aboard. Crystal stood up and wobbled a little until she found her new center of gravity. Her face turned an instant red when Len wrapped her tiny arms around her throat too tightly.

"Loosen up, Len," said Noe.

"Sorry," said Len, and moved her hands to Crystal's forehead.

"Everyone knows their places tonight?" asked Noe.

"I'm on the kitchen side of the house," said Crystal.

"I'm on the garage side," said Radiah.

"And I'll stick close to Len," said Noe.

"And I'm on Crystal's head," said Len, putting her hands over Crystal's eyes and laughing.

More neighbors were walking down the street now, laden with bags of chips and bottles of soda and pans and plates and bowls full of homemade food. "Let's go party, I guess," said Noe, and the four girls headed to the backyard on six legs.

It was impossible to enjoy themselves. Even though they didn't have to do anything until dusk, the weight of what they were going to try hovered over the backyard like it was about to drop and flatten them all into smashed people. The watched the fire build into a giant raging cone, but it wasn't as interesting as it would otherwise have been. The smell of grilling steaks and corn wasn't tempting. The tables full of desserts were easy to ignore. Seeing so many people around wasn't exciting. The Dread Enders just kept waiting for night to fall.

The girls ended up hanging out at the edge of the yard at Wombat Rock—Len's name for it had caught on. It was a mossy hump of granite about the size of a teacher's desk, about half the size of Rune Rock, and not at all shaped like its namesake. Wombat Rock was far enough away from the party to stop adults from coming up and asking them questions about school or the handles sticking out of their pockets or offering their condolences about Ruthy, but not so far away that they were too isolated.

The girls took turns giving Len piggyback rides, but mostly they kept their eyes on the forest. And the backyard. And the fence that divided them from their neighbor on the one side. They had no idea what direction the Smashed Man would come from. Mostly the girls leaned against the rock, ate chips, and swatted at the flies swimming through the hazy heat.

Eventually somebody handed out s'mores sticks, and Noe took Len to get one. Crystal and Radiah followed, although cautiously. If the s'mores sticks were being brandished, it was almost nightfall.

Finally dusk coated the sky enough for the bats to come out, circling above them and around the Pilgrim weather vane like they did every night, flapping like mad and gorging gleefully on hordes of tiny insects. The girls took up their positions, Radiah on one side of the house, Crystal on the other, and Noe close to the back door with Len beside her.

Len panicked right on schedule. At least one part of their plan was predictable.

"It's dark," said Len to her sister, a sticky, crumbly

remnant of s'more squeezed in one of her small hands, the kiwi bird dangling from the other. "Werewolves will come."

"Yeah, they might." Noe felt bad as soon as she said it. But she had to.

"I want to go inside." Len was panicking. "I want to go inside." She dropped the rest of the s'more into the grass, instantly forgotten. "I want to go inside."

"Okay, okay. Hold on." Noe looked around the backyard and saw Dad throwing a log on the bonfire and talking to Radiah's dad, who was tall and bald and looked strong enough to lift her father with one arm. She walked over to her dad, pulling Len behind. "Dad, Len's panicking about the dark. I'm going to take her inside, let her play on my laptop for a while."

"Sure. Thanks, honey." He went back to his discussion with Mr. Harris.

Noe led Len across the yard and into the house through the back screen door. She stopped at the kitchen sink to help her wash the marshmallow and chocolate off her hands and the kiwi bird, and then started leading her up the stairs to her room.

"I don't want to go to my room," said Len, yanking her hand back from Noe's.

"It's only for a little while, until the bonfire is over.

And you get to play on my laptop."

"I'll be all alone in there," said Len.

"You have to go in there. Or my room. Do you want to stay in my room?"

"No. I don't want to be alone."

"You'll have your animals. . . ."

Len thought about it. "Can I have all my animals in your room with your laptop?"

"Len, I don't have time . . ." But Len had crossed her arms across her kiwi bird and was standing firm on her terms.

"Okay. Let's get them in there fast, though." Len broke out in a large smile and beat her big sister upstairs with an "I win!" Noe didn't have time for this, but she really needed Len as far away from what was about to happen as possible, and to be protected behind a door. The two girls started transferring stuffed animals by the armload from Len's room into Noe's like they were playing Noah's Ark. It took five trips to get them all moved. Noe's bed was now three feet taller with all the animals on it. Len dived in.

Noe got Len set up on the laptop with a bunch of games and videos she liked. "You have to make a promise to me." Len didn't answer. She was already engrossed in a video. Noe shut the laptop.

"Hey!" said Len.

"You have to promise me something."

"Okay."

"In a little bit, me and Crystal and Radiah will be downstairs in the kitchen. You might hear us shouting, but you cannot leave this room. It's very important that you stay here until I come and get you."

"Okay."

"I'm serious." Noe paused and then said, "Or the werewolves will get you." Len's eyes widened and she wrapped her arms around a pangolin. Noe opened the laptop, and Len was immediately distracted by it.

Noe closed the door and went downstairs. She opened a cabinet in the kitchen and dipped her brush in the bucket of darkwash that she had hidden there. Tiptoeing back upstairs, she painted a quick Amberonk on her door.

With Len safe, Noe headed back outside. It was full night out there. She made eye contact with Crystal and Radiah, who were still at their posts, although looking more worried, and then took up her post beside the back door and waited.

Noe dipped her paintbrush into the darkwash that she'd hidden by the back-door stairs and held it at the ready. She strained her eyes so hard into the darkness that her head started aching. From where Crystal and Radiah stood on each side of the house, they could see both the front lawn and the street, as well as the backyard. They alternated their attention between the two views.

As Noe stood within arm's reach of the Amberonk on the back of the house, she automatically grabbed the Elberex dangling from her neck. She had to hide it under her shirt most of the time, otherwise her parents' eyes went purple every time they looked at her, like she was the Smashed Man. With all the adults blind to what was going on in this neighborhood, it was almost like she was living in an imaginary world of her own creation.

At eight forty-five, there was still no Smashed Man. It was all Noe could do to not run screaming into the forest.

Every once in a while, an adult walked by, their eyes flashing purple when they looked in the direction of the sigil on the house as they said hi to Noe or asked her why she was holding a paintbrush in the air. The Amberonk sparkled like crazy with reflected firelight, almost making it more visible now than it was during the day. The effect was mesmerizing. She stared at the darkwash sigil for a long time. Too long. She almost missed the Smashed Man.

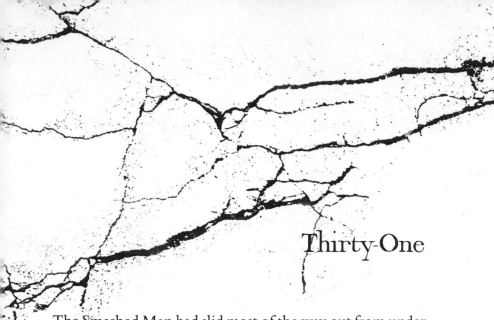

# Thirty-One

The Smashed Man had slid most of the way out from under Wombat Rock when she saw him. Noe shuddered, realizing that he had been right beneath them.

It was time to act.

She looked over at Crystal and then at Radiah, neither of whom seemed to have noticed yet. "Radiah! Crystal! Now!" she shouted. Half of the adults in the yard looked at her, but only briefly. Kids and kids yelling were the same things to them. Noe pointed her gloppy paintbrush at where the Smashed Man wavered and bounced at the edge of the yard. She waited for a shout from an adult or for one of the small groups spread across the lawn to run in alarm, but of course that didn't happen. The summer bonfire continued like there wasn't a monster there.

The Smashed Man moved.

He slid through the crowd, all purple eyed and oblivious

to the horror weaving and wavering among them. His eyes were glowing purple dots, and the darkwash stains on his face reflected the firelight, giving him a grotesque glittery mask.

He was headed straight for Noe.

Radiah and Crystal were also headed for Noe, their paintbrushes at the ready.

Noe kept eye contact with the Smashed Man. She wanted to make sure he focused on her and not on Crystal and Radiah. He was coming at her fast. She could see the reddish rips in the skin of his face and body. See the gleaming of his teeth in the bonfire light, the ever-present grin making her skin goose-bump like it wanted to pull from her body. His flat head never turned to the left or the right. He completely ignored the crowd of adults he was sliding through, and the adults did the same.

She heard the screen door slam behind her, meaning Radiah and Crystal were now safely inside and protected by the Amberonks on the house.

Noe was alone in a backyard full of oblivious revelers.

She reached back with her brush and painted a few slashes over the Amberonk with fresh darkwash, destroying the old sigil.

The back of the house was no longer protected.

Noe readied herself as the Smashed Man drew closer. He was to the bonfire now.

No, he was in the bonfire. The Smashed Man wavered and floated and undulated inside the giant fiery cone. For a moment he paused, the skewered marshmallows so close to his face he could have bitten them off their sticks, and the adults, completely ignorant and purple eyed, surrounding the fire and chatting warmly with drinks in their hands as their marshmallows browned. The flames lit up the dark-wash stains on the monster's face furiously but could not mute the shimmering of his violet irises. His mask of madness never twitched, even as the flames roared around him and then soared above him as cinders and smoke rose into the bat-filled night sky.

And then he walked out of the bonfire, unsinged, untouched by the flames, indestructible. If fire couldn't hurt him, then what hope did three girls with paintbrushes have? Noe's knees almost buckled in fear and disappointment.

"Hello, everyone!" A loud voice cut across the murmur of people around the bonfire. "Sorry I'm late!" It was Mrs. Washington. She was walking into the backyard with a casserole dish and a small boy who looked to be Ruthy's age. "This is my grandson. He's staying with me for the weekend."

Noe looked back at the Smashed Man. His head twisted like a cobra's to take in the boy. His body twisted in the same direction, and he started running right for him, weaving through the adults, who clutched paper plates and drinks and talked while the monster moved inches away from them.

Noe also charged at the boy. "Hi, Mrs. Washington! I'll take him to where all the kids are playing! Let's go!" She grabbed the boy's hand and started pulling him toward the house. The boy didn't say anything, just looked back at his grandmother in confusion. Noe didn't bother to gauge where the Smashed Man was. It didn't matter. It only mattered that she make it through the back door. And then after that, all kinds of other things mattered.

"His name is Ben!" Mrs. Washington called after her. "And I promised him s'mores!"

Radiah and Crystal were holding the back door open and yelling at her to hurry, like the night she had thrown the bucket of darkwash in the Smashed Man's face. But she hadn't been pulling a boy behind her that time. Ben wasn't fighting her, but he wasn't following as fast as he should be. Not like his life depended on it. "Faster, Ben!" she yelled.

Finally Noe dived through the door, pulling Ben behind her, who happened to look over his shoulder as they crossed the threshold. He screamed when he finally saw the Smashed Man bearing down on them. Radiah slammed the door shut.

"Girls, take it easy on that door!" Noe heard Dad yell from outside.

Crystal had already grabbed the bucket of darkwash hidden in the cabinet and was now standing against the back wall of the kitchen. Radiah dipped her brush into Crystal's bucket before rushing over to the half-open basement door. Noe, who according to the plan was supposed to join Radiah, instead pulled the screaming boy through the kitchen and into the living room. She pushed Ben onto the couch and said, "Don't move and don't make a sound or that monster will get you." Ben whimpered into silence.

Noe made it back to the kitchen just as a flat head slipped beneath the door beside where Crystal was standing. Radiah was nowhere to be seen. Crystal was pushing back against the wall so hard it seemed like she was trying to phase through it and escape the house.

The flat head bent up and leered at them. Noe wanted to kick it in the face. But she knew what touching the Smashed Man would do to her. Plus it wasn't time for attacking.

"Get ready, Crystal," said Noe. Crystal nodded and adjusted the bucket and paintbrush in her hands.

Noe looked over at the basement door. It was wide open now. Although Noe couldn't see Radiah, she knew that her friend was hiding on the other side of the door, keeping it open and herself out of sight of the Smashed Man. Not because she was scared, although she probably was, but because it was her job. Noe moved over so that her back was in front of the open basement door and she was facing the Smashed Man.

He oozed quickly under the screen door and stood up in the kitchen, undulating and wavering and staring right at Noe, who didn't move.

Crystal quickly painted an Amberonk on the back kitchen wall. The Smashed Man turned his flat head toward her, but his body stayed framed up to Noe. Crystal lifted the bucket of darkwash threateningly and backed away toward the living room, getting ready, if she had to, to dash in there to grab Ben and continue running around the loop of the first floor and out the front door, where the Smashed Man couldn't follow because of the Amberonk on the front of the house. He was now trapped in Noe's house, whether he realized it or not. He turned back to Noe.

Noe slowly backed toward the stairs. The Smashed Man came toward her. The second she was sure he was committed, Noe turned around and ran down the steps.

The Smashed Man followed her down.

Radiah slammed the basement door shut, a paintbrush in her hand and a dripping Amberonk painted on the door.

The Smashed Man was trapped in the basement.

With Noe.

This was how the whole thing had started for her. The

basement, an impossible monster, and her. This was also where it was going to end. Where it was always going to end, whether through her sleepwalking down here, or this way, as part of a desperate plan.

The usual oppressiveness of the thick walls and dim air and dirt floor of the basement was almost comforting to her now. She could imagine Erica sitting on the dryer, writing in her diary, getting ready to face the Smashed Man. Noe drew strength from that image, felt less alone. She was determined to do what Erica hadn't been able to do, even though she had tried: to protect her friends from the monster permanently.

Noe wasn't scared right now. Any type of scared. She circled around to put the water heater between her and the Smashed Man. And then she realized that she wasn't the only one trapped in the basement with the Smashed Man.

"Len!" she screamed.

Len was standing in the corner, a stuffed anaconda wrapped around her neck like a scarf, swaying with her eyes closed.

She was sleepwalking.

Len must have fallen asleep upstairs. Now Noe was scared. The worst kind of scared. The scared-for-somebody-you-love kind of scared. "Len!" Noe screamed again, running over to her sister and shaking her. It didn't do anything. She pushed Len deeper into the corner, watching the Smashed Man slither down the steps on his stomach, his head up the entire time and focused on the sisters.

The Smashed Man rose slowly from the ground until he was standing in the dimness. He didn't need to move so slow, Noe knew. He hadn't been slow since he escaped the crack into their world. He was enjoying her terror. The Smashed Man took a few wobbly steps across the hard-packed dirt. His grin, bright against his darkwashed countenance, almost ripped his face in two. There was no way she could race past him and get back up the stairs to safety, even without Len. He was too fast and would grab her easily.

Noe stepped forward, keeping herself between the flat monster and her sister.

She waited for him to come closer.

Waited for him to get so close that she could see the texture in his shining purple irises.

And finally, and for not the first time since she had moved to Dread End, she was within breathing distance of the Smashed Man.

She let him reach out, started to feel electric tingles as his flat fingers neared her skin.

And then she lifted her fist.

Wrapped around it was the leather cord that had been

around her neck all night. It held the solid Elberex tight against the flat of her fist like a set of brass knuckles.

She hit him right across the eyes as hard as she could. It was violent. It was satisfying. It felt far from silly. It felt like what needed to be done. What Erica had been so close to figuring out.

The Smashed Man staggered backward, and for only the second time, she saw the Smashed Man's expression change. It wrinkled into surprise and pain, the leer completely gone. Instead of the Elberex being painted on his forehead like the last time, the Elberex was branded around his eyes like she had held the sigil in the bonfire for hours. She smelled burning chemicals. The shimmering purple was gone, like his eyes had been smashed inward. All that was above his cruelly gaping mouth was the black double shape of the Elberex's mark, smoke wafting from it like a wet coal.

Noe felt a pain in her hand, and she looked down and saw smoke rising from the Elberex and felt it burning through the leather cord. She flung it from her hand to the dirt. The Smashed Man tried to step forward toward Noe, but bent over instead, like she had hit him in the gut. He started levitating into the air. Halfway between the dirt and the rafters, he continued to bend, until he twisted in the middle and crossed over himself, like the snake in her nightmares, his face ending up at his feet. He was floating in the basement in the shape of the Elberex, a Möbius strip turning in on himself, and then, like the Elberex in her meditation dream, he was continuing to turn in on himself, spinning faster and faster in that shape, through the twin loops like he was on a roller-coaster track.

Noe stumbled back to Len and pushed her to the floor, shielding her with her body. The air was buzzing and strange and she thought for sure the Smashed Man was about to explode and bring the whole house down on top of them. Noe heard a painful rip and a horrible scream, and she couldn't help but glance up. She saw the Smashed Man Elberex coming apart, dissolving into particles, like the centrifugal force of his twisting was ripping him in pieces. Noe's head felt like it was being crushed by a dozen hands. A sound like a hard wind moved through the basement.

And then everything stilled.

Noe took her hands from around her sister and looked at the basement. The Smashed Man was gone, like he had been torn right out of the universe, out of existence, out of their lives. Everything was silent except for a slight hum in her ears.

The atmosphere in the basement had changed. Like the house had been moved a few altitudes higher, or scrubbed clean by ozone and electricity. Noe looked down and saw her sister waking up. She looked at the other side of the basement and saw Crystal and Radiah on the stairs looking dazed, like they had been the ones sleepwalking.

"Did you see that?" asked Noe.

Radiah nodded.

"Is he gone?" asked Crystal.

"Noe? Len? Where are you guys?" Mom came down the steps. "What's going on here? Mrs. Washington's grandson just came outside crying about a monster. What did you girls tell him? And why are you down here?"

Noe dropped her arms, exhausted. The hum in her ears had stopped, and she was happy to hear a normal voice and a normal question that meant the world was normal again. Happy to see Mom's deep green eyes. She hugged Len to her chest, who was rubbing at her eyes dazedly and mumbling, "Werewolves. Werewolves."

"That's right, Len. Werewolves. The boy couldn't handle the werewolves." Noe turned to Mom. "Len was sleepwalking. But she's all right now."

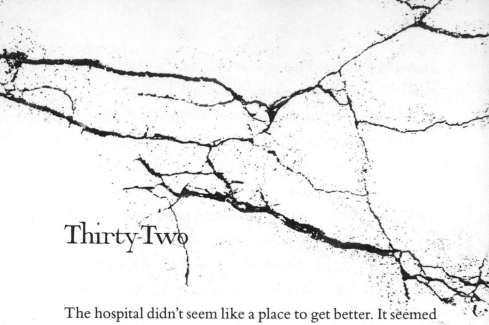

# Thirty-Two

The hospital didn't seem like a place to get better. It seemed like a place to disappear. The walls were white and beige, and the hallways seemed to go on forever past identical-looking rooms with identical-looking beds inside. The three girls had walked those never-ending halls to a small waiting room with small brown couches, where they sat, waiting.

The girls didn't speak. It didn't seem like a place to speak. Crystal was staring at a painting of a nun with large eyes that hung on the wall. Radiah was tugging on the witch stone around her neck and focusing on the open door. She had a plastic grocery bag on her lap that was bulging with sharp corners. Noe reached up and felt the comforting shape of the Elberex through her shirt. It hung on a black metal chain around her neck. The three girls looked like they were lined up outside the principal's office, except every once in a while, Crystal's lips stretched like she was fighting back a smile. She was unfamiliar with what it was like to sit outside a principal's office.

After what seemed like half of their lives, a nurse leaned into the doorway of the waiting room. She was dressed in loose green scrubs and wore glasses with matching green frames. She motioned at the girls with two fingers, and the girls got up and followed her. They walked down another white-and-beige hall full of identical rooms with identical beds.

The nurse stopped at one of the doors, which was open, although a curtain blocked their view inside. She stuck her head in past the curtain. "You've got visitors," she sang, and then turned and winked at the girls before wandering off down the other side of the everlasting hallway.

Radiah led the way into the room, lifting the curtain uncertainly.

Ruthy had always looked tiny, but the giant hospital bed she was sitting in made her look infinitesimal. A tray beside her was full of empty Jell-O cups, and a TV on the wall blared toy commercials. Her blond hair looked greasy, and she had a red pimple on her cheek.

"Ruthy!" screamed Radiah, and like the word was a starting whistle at a race, all three girls ran at the little girl until the four were a jostling mass of hugs and falling

Jell-O cups and giggling and bed squeaks and crying. Noe lost herself in the moment, only remembering after it was over that these were all girls she had only met a couple of months ago.

"We're so glad you're okay!" said Radiah.

"We were so worried," said Crystal.

"Look, we brought you something." Radiah reached into the plastic bag and pulled out a thick stack of colorful construction paper wrapped in plastic, a new box of crayons, and a pair of scissors that still had the tag on it.

Ruthy's forehead crinkled. "You don't like it when I make the Smashed Man."

Radiah's smile almost jumped off her face. "You don't need to make the Smashed Man anymore. You can make anything you want." Radiah looked at Noe and Crystal. They nodded her on, matching smiles on their faces. "He's gone . . ." Radiah's voice hitched before she got out the last word. "Forever."

Ruthy's eyes widened and she looked at each girl in turn, as if testing the idea on their faces, looking for the first change in their smiles, the first "Just kidding!" from their lips. "What? How?"

They told Ruthy the whole story, each telling a part until another couldn't hold it in any longer and interrupted. Ruthy held both her hands in the air above the stack of construction paper, as if trying to manage the story with her hands. "You did it? You beat him?"

"Thanks to Noe," said Radiah, elbowing Noe in the side.

"It was my fault that he was out in the first place," said Noe, looking at Ruthy. "My fault you're even in here. Do you remember what happened that night?"

Ruthy shook her head. "I remember seeing him above me. And then nightmares. Lots of nightmares. White faces with dark eyes. An orange sky. I feel like I've been away a long time."

Noe almost jumped when Ruthy mentioned the faces. She tried to hide her surprise by saying, "Do the doctors have any idea what happened to you?"

Ruthy shrugged. "I don't know. They just tell me that I'm doing good." She opened and closed the scissors in front of her a few times. "Am I awake because the Smashed Man is gone?"

The other three girls looked at each other like they were dreading the question. "We don't know," said Radiah.

"Does that mean Erica's all right?" That was the question they were actually dreading.

Crystal and Radiah looked at each other, both trying to hold back powerful emotions. They had already had this conversation and had convinced Radiah's mom to call Erica's, hoping for good news. "No," said Radiah.

"What's that?" Noe pointed to a mark on the pale skin

above Ruthy's elbow. It was pink and looked like a vertical line with another line twisting around it, like the silhouette of a vine around a pole.

"I don't know," said Ruthy, shifting her arm so that she could see the mark. "I hadn't noticed it before."

Noe kept staring at it. "I don't think Ruthy's awake because we got rid of the Smashed Man."

"Why do you say that?" asked Crystal.

"Because we've seen that sigil before," said Noe.

"It's the eckolong," said Fern. "It can heal, although under what conditions we still don't quite know. It was a guess using it on that little girl in the coma."

Fern and Noe were once more in the living room of the white house, drinking tea out of elephant cups. Noe was almost . . . almost . . . starting to enjoy these moments in this secret hideout with this grouchy woman on the edge of a universe that boggled her mind. But it was mostly the tea.

"A guess or an experiment?" Noe asked.

"Is there a difference?"

"Have you ever used the sigil before?"

"No. We've known about the sigil itself, but I only learned what it could do when I met with the Neighbors. Another member had discovered its purpose. But making it solid really increased the power of its properties. Pulled that little girl right out of her coma as soon as I touched her with it."

"So this can help Erica?"

Fern took a long sip of her tea, long enough to drink what was in that cup three times over. "We already tried it on the girl in Texas. It didn't work."

Noe felt her belly drop. She had kind of expected that answer.

"How are those two girls doing with that book?" Fern asked.

Fern wanted the girls to record everything about the Smashed Man and what had happened over the past couple of months in their own words. The Dread Enders had nominated Crystal to do it, since she had already started with her yellow notebook. Radiah was doing illustrations for it.

"I think they're almost done."

"Are you still meditating?"

"Yes." Noe had found a great place to meditate—her basement. She had no reason to fear the place now, and the noise of the washer and dryer relaxed her and covered up her oms. "I haven't seen anything new."

"There are other reasons to meditate. I bet you haven't had any parasomnia episodes since you started."

Noe looked at her in surprise. Fern was right. She hadn't sleepwalked or had any nightmares in a while. "It made them go away?"

"I don't know about that. But it at least channels them in some way. You, like all children, have a sensitivity to stuck places. And you happen to be more sensitive than most. That girl in Texas was too. I don't think it was any coincidence you both lived in the same house."

"What do you mean?"

"I think you were drawn here. Pulled to a neighborhood where a place got stuck and the barrier between them thinned." Noe remembered that she had been the one who had found the house. "But you'll need to be careful."

"Why?" asked Noe, confused because with the Smashed Man gone, it was finally the time to not be careful.

"You never asked me what the Neighbors call the Smashed Man."

"You had your own name for him?"

"Long before you girls did."

That surprised her, although it shouldn't have. "What was it?"

"Matt."

Noe waited for Fern to laugh. She didn't. "Is that a joke? Like flat as a door mat?"

"Nooo." Fern drew out the word. "That's his name. Matthew Impey. He was a Neighbor."

Noe had never considered the Smashed Man a person before, even though he looked like one. The idea horrified her more than the Smashed Man being an interdimensional monster. "What happened to him?" She almost didn't want to know.

"He fell through a weak spot where the stuck place touched our own. We think it's happened before, elsewhere. Sometimes people disappear and are never found. Maybe they fall through the universe. Into the space between stuck places. It should kill them, and probably does more often than not, but sometimes it . . . changes them. Turns them into creatures of torment and rage and violence."

"There's more than one Smashed Man?"

Fern nodded, adjusting her red glasses. "I'm not trying to scare you. Well, I am, but for good reason. I'm bringing it up because Matthew Impey was special. Extremely sensitive to stuck places. He's the one who discovered the darkwash. He also did the foundational work on the sigils."

"I thought you said the sigils have always been around. Like in Egypt." Noe grabbed at the Elberex hanging around her neck.

"They've always been around in human consciousness and culture, but their properties as elements that affect the particles of existence had to be discovered through cell knowledge. Just like how to make darkwash and how to make darkstuff. That's what I'm calling solid darkwash, by the way. What do you think?"

Noe shrugged.

"I guess it's no 'Rune Rock' or 'Smashed Man.' But

listen to me, girl. Matthew Impey got too close to the stuck place. He was a genius at uncovering knowledge about it, but that affinity with the stuck place caused his tragedy. There's still a stuck place under this neighborhood, and you, in particular, should be careful." She took a sip of chai. "Not that I care. Overly, anyway."

Noe didn't like where this was going. She put her teacup down. "I've got to get back to my house." She got up, opened the front door, and stopped. She did this every time she left the white house. She loved looking at the neighborhood when it couldn't look back at her. Especially now. Totter Court felt different these days. Sunnier. More open. Like a giant bubble that had been encasing the neighborhood had popped. Even if it still sat on top of a stuck place.

"I guess you're going back to Gulf Shores now?" Noe asked without turning around.

"I wish. Thanks to you girls, I'm going to be here for a little while longer." She sounded like she wanted to throw her entire tea service across the room.

Noe turned around. "What do you mean? There's no reason for you to be here anymore. We got rid of the Smashed Man."

"That's the problem."

"I don't understand."

"I have to stick around to see what comes out of the crack in your basement next."

# Acknowledgments

One of the hardest things about being an author is the hours spent alone toiling away on a story. But if you're fortunate, it leads to one of the best things about being an author, gaining a team that believes in your story enough to help you bring it to the world. And I have a great team.

My oldest daughter, Esme, was the first to read this book. If she hadn't liked it, I would have spiked it instantly. The same with my wife, Lindsey, who not only helps me with early drafts but also has to put up with my writing process itself, and I am forever grateful for that. My friend John Rozum offered suggestions that inspired a key image that became my favorite in the book. I'm not sure I have the confidence to send out a manuscript without my friend Christian Haunton reading it first, as his care and discernment with my manuscripts always makes my ideas more meaningful. My agent, Alex Slater, gave me both story help in the beginning, when it was just an idea, and business help in the end, when it was just a Word file. He's worked miracles with every manuscript I've given him.

My editor, Elizabeth Lynch, is the reason this book is in your hands. She believed in this strange, complex little story with its strange monster from the start, helped me improve it, and brought some amazing talent together at HarperCollins to create the book, including Laaren Brown, Renée Cafiero, and Alexandra Rakaczki for their painstaking and valuable scrutiny of the manuscript and Jeannette Arroyo, Catherine Lee, and Alison Klapthor for the gorgeous, ominous cover.